RIGHT PRYCE WRONG TIME

BRENDA BARRETT

Right Pryce Wrong Time

A Jamaica Treasures Book/September 2019
Published by Jamaica Treasures
Kingston, Jamaica

978-976-8247-71-1
Jamaica Treasures
P.O. Box 482
Kingston 19
Jamaica W.I.
www.fiwibooks.com

She was staring, she couldn't drag her eyes away. This was how it had started all those years ago.

He had walked into the classroom, and her heart had taken flight beating at an irregular rate, and everything else had faded around her. She had become hyper-aware of herself, of her feelings. It was as if everything else ceased to exist when James Dalton was in the same room with her.

The feeling was back.

She inhaled raggedly.

Yup, here was the spark. The feeling that had eluded her for six years, the feeling that she wished she had even a tiny iota of for Cole. It was back in full force.

Then his eyes met hers. How could they not?

In the past, when she had stared at him long enough, he had always turned around to look at her too. Back then, she was met with stony rejection. This time, he didn't drag his eyes away.

This time, he held her gaze...

ALSO BY BRENDA BARRETT

FULL CIRCLE
NEW BEGINNINGS
THE PREACHER AND THE PROSTITUTE
AFTER THE END
THE EMPTY HAMMOCK
THE PULL OF FREEDOM
REBOUND SERIES
THREE RIVERS SERIES
NEW SONG SERIES
BANCROFT SERIES
MAGNOLIA SISTERS SERIES
SCARLETT SERIES
WILEY BROTHERS SERIES

ABOUT THE AUTHOR

Books have always been a big part of life for Jamaican born Brenda Barrett, she reports that she gets withdrawal symptoms if she does not consume at least two books per week. That is all she can manage these days, as her days are filled with writing, a natural progression from her love of reading. Currently, Brenda has several novels on the market, she writes predominantly in the historical fiction, Christian fiction, comedy and romance genres.

Apart from writing fictional books, Brenda writes for her blogs blackhair101.com; where she gives hair care tips and fiwibooks.com, where she shares about her writing life.

You can connect with Brenda online at:
Brenda-Barrett.com
Twitter.com/AuthorWriterBB
Facebook.com/AuthorBrendaBarrett

Chapter One

"Tiana Pryce, you will not believe this!" Carla entered the office that they shared, waving a piece of paper.

"What?" Tiana looked up from her laptop. She was editing the most boring law textbook ever written. The professor who wrote it seriously hated his students and wanted them to suffer.

"My cousin Minka, who works at JD Productions in California, just gave me the best news! The best!"

"She won the lottery, and she is giving you half?" Tiana grinned. "Congrats!"

"No." Carla chuckled. "That would be good news, but I don't like free money. I like to work for it, but this news is like winning the lottery."

"Okay, I'll bite." Tiana grinned. "What is it?"

"I am so happy I cannot speak! I need this to sink in." Carla plopped herself in her chair and pinched herself. "Tell me this is not a dream!"

"It's not a dream," Tiana said, leaning forward in her chair. "I can't wait to hear what has you so breathlessly excited."

Carla fanned herself dramatically. The air conditioner was high enough that fanning was unnecessary, but Carla seemed like she needed to do something with her hands. She was hyperventilating.

Carla took a deep breath and then another. "Okay, so, I didn't tell you this, but I've been sending Minka scripts to sneak into her boss. She's a production assistant on the show Secrets of Love."

"Which you are obsessed with." Tiana supplied.

"It finally worked; the writers are going to use one of my scripts for season five!" Carla said in a rush. "They want to fly me over there to work on season five with them. Me, Carla Lindsay! I am gonna work on Secrets of Love. My words will be in the mouths of the actors. My thoughts will be brought to life. My name will be on the screen!"

"Are you serious?" Tiana squealed. "Seriously!"

"Yes." Carla gasped. "I absolutely can't believe it.

"You will have to pause the credits at the end to see your name." Tiana said enviously, "but still, that's great. A writer's dream. My dream."

"I know." Carla blinked her eyes rapidly. "I am… what's that word that Mr. Oliver likes to use?"

"Gobsmacked," Tiana said faintly. "Wow, I am jealous and happy for you at the same time."

"No need for jealousy, Missy." Carla smiled. "I have good news for you too."

"They want me to work on Secrets of Love?" Tiana widened her eyes. "I don't even watch the show anymore. I stopped when they killed off the hotel doctor. He was the one who was solving all the clues. He was the reason why I watched it in the first place."

"He was a villain." Carla grinned. "They have a new villain every season. Anyway, they brought him back as his twin brother, and it is even juicier than season two, the twin brother was seeing the hotel manager."

"Goodness." Tiana grinned. "Talk about a plot twist."

"Anyway," Carla said, "we were talking about your good news."

"Yes." Tiana nodded eagerly.

"A new mini-series is going to be filmed here in Jamaica. Minka said it's a period piece. I don't know what it's about, and I don't know where the filming location will be, but the showrunner for Secrets of Love is in Jamaica to join the writing team for that show."

"Get out of here!" Tiana gasped. "That's awesome."

"Yup." Carla nodded. "I am almost persuaded to give up my beloved Secrets of Love for this new project, but the thing is, I am not sure if I would get a shoo-in for this. Minka said more than forty writers have already applied for it, and they only need two from the pool. It will be a rigorous interview process, and apparently you have to know 1800s Jamaican history."

Tiana made a face. "There goes my hopes. I am just an amateur I won't get a shoo-in."

"Don't say that yet." Carla handed her the paper. "They are still taking manuscripts to assess who should be shortlisted. Unfortunately, today is the deadline."

Tiana took the paper from her and scanned it. "You have to send a sample of your writing to Traci Pink at JD Productions?"

"Yup, that's the showrunner's assistant." Carla nodded, "Minka says she is brutal. Then you are required to spend three weeks somewhere in St. Ann where they put you through a series of pressure tests and writing obstacles where one person will be eliminated until they reach the final two."

Tiana looked up. "What kind of a job interview is this?"

"Sounds good to me," Carla said. "They have to be thorough, make sure that you can work with the writing team or that you can actually write. It's a great opportunity. I'd do it just for the competition."

"Yes, I know you love competition." Tiana frowned, "but I don't."

"You must enter. Send them that novella that you wrote about the teacher. It shows off your awesome writing skills," Carla insisted. "Every day you complain about your job here. Neither of us like non-fiction work."

Tiana blushed. "I er think it needs work."

"It was good. I liked it. Once upon a time when Cannon Publishers took fiction manuscripts, I edited those." Carla grinned. "I think your story would sell. Take a chance, T. You shouldn't miss this opportunity. I know how miserable you have been lately."

"It's these law journals." Tiana rubbed the back of her neck. "I don't mind editing. I love it but this past year I've been editing one dry, thirsty, thousand-page journal after the other. Besides, there is no way Mr. Oliver is going to give me three weeks' vacation. I took a week to see my sister run in Europe. He grumbled the whole time he was signing off on it."

"And though I am almost done with this boring monstrosity of a law book. I have the history tomes to get through. It's three volumes, and I have to double-check dates and all of that…"

"So quit your job," Carla said flippantly.

"Quit my job." Tiana widened her eyes. "Quit my job! Are you crazy? I am saving up to buy a house."

"You can always come back with your tail between your

legs if you fail." Carla rolled her eyes. "You know, Mr. Oliver has a soft spot for you. We have more manuscripts than editors for the next two years and this place could always use one more editor, but you should chase that dream."

Tiana shook her head. "I don't know. I'll think about it."

"The deadline to enter is today." Carla pointed at the paper. "You don't have a lot of time to think about it."

Tiana drummed her fingers on the desk. "Well…"

"It takes a lot of courage to release the familiar and seemingly secure, to embrace the new. But there is no real security in what is no longer meaningful. There is more security in the adventurous and exciting, for in movement, there is life, and in change, there is power." Carla read the quote she had posted above her desk.

"Andy Cohen knew what he was talking about." She flashed a grin at Tiana. "That's why I am quitting too. I've already typed up the resignation letter."

Tiana grunted. "I am not you, Carla. I don't know, I don't know…"

"You will get past round one," Carla said encouragingly. "Enter the thing, send your teacher script. If they call you for the three-week interview, go. Simple. You have to be in it to win it."

Tiana grabbed the paper again and typed off the email address. "I guess it won't hurt to send the sample. I can always beg for the three weeks from Mr. Oliver. That way if I am booted in the elimination round, I still have a job to return to."

"Yes, that's the spirit. Send it then forget about it," Carla said, "I'll have to make plans to hand off my pile of manuscripts and alert HR to my imminent resignation."

"You know, I have been working with you for a year, but you never struck me as the type of person who would pull up stakes and leave it all behind."

Carla laughed. "People always read me wrong. I have a bookish air about me, but under this nerd exterior there is a rabid adventuress. I am thirty-nine and single. Nothing is holding me back. I say seize the day."

"Seize the day." Tiana turned to her computer. "Okay, I am seizing the day. Carpe diem."

"I heard that the showrunner of Secrets of Love is scrumptious," Carla said after she sent the manuscript. "Minka says he is especially lovely to look at. How did she put it? He has the prettiest green eyes, the purest caramel complexion, and the pinkest most sensual lips. She thinks he should be in front of the camera, not behind it."

Tiana hit send and then jerked. That description could fit James Dalton, she thought.

"What's his name?" She asked her voice coming out in a croak.

"I don't remember." Carla said dreamily, "I was trying to envision what the combination of green eyes, dark skin, and pink lips would look like. Maybe Jesse Williams, that doctor from Grey's Anatomy? His eyes are green, right?"

"Don't remember," Tiana groaned. "Try to recall, Carla. What was the name of this showrunner?"

Carla closed her eyes dramatically.

"Was it, James?" Tiana looked at the monitor fearfully.

"Yes, that's right." Carla nodded. "James David, or was it, James Derrick. It was two first names."

"James Dalton." Tiana slumped in her chair, "JD Productions. Oh my word, I shouldn't have sent my manuscript then."

"Why not?" Carla asked. "Do you know James Dalton?"

"Oh, yes." Tiana nodded. "He was my high school English teacher."

"That's great!" Carla grinned. "Were you a good student?"

"Well," Tiana bit her lips, "I would write the most elaborate essays."

"He'll shortlist you in a heartbeat then." Carla clapped, "You are his former student, how could he not?"

"Well," Tiana shook her head, "the essays I wrote were about him and me, some of them were pretty cheesy and outright erotic. I stalked him, got him fired from his job when I got one of my friends to take a picture of us kissing."

Carla widened her eyes. "What?"

"I had a gigantic crush on the man." Tiana sighed. "Let me tell you, I had it bad. I had this idea to take a picture of us kissing, but then my phone got lost, and the principal of all people was the one who found it. She scrolled through my pictures hoping to identify whose phone it was, and what do you think she saw, one of her teachers in a compromising position with her student. He was fired the same day."

"Wow, that's tough." Carla shook her head. "Did he kiss you back?"

"No." Tiana groaned. "He was shocked at first, and then he was mad, especially when he saw Yara with my phone snapping away. I have never seen a person angrier than Mr. Dalton was that day. He thought I was out to ruin him.

"He hates me.

"Might as well get back to this law journal because there is no hope of me getting chosen for his writing team. Once he sees my name, my work is going to file-thirteen without a doubt."

Chapter Two

Tiana fretted about her application after she spoke to Carla. There was no way she could concentrate on her work now. She had always been a little sensitive where James Dalton was concerned.

She had made a royal fool of herself over him when she was in high school, and her sisters never let her forget it. Her best friend Yara was always bringing him up. She claimed that James Dalton was the measuring stick for all her relationships.

Tiana denied it vehemently, but she knew it was true. She subconsciously compared every man that came into her life to her high school teacher. How weird was that? It's as if all her passion, her zeal, her intensity had been so focused on the one man she had run out of those particular emotions as an adult.

Nobody could get her excited again, and she had tried. She had dated quite a lot in university. She had even drifted into a two-year relationship with a perfectly suitable man. A man who was serious about her and had asked her to marry him a month ago.

She couldn't tell him yes.

Something was missing between them, and she didn't know how to explain it to Cole. He was a catch, everyone knew it, and everyone told her how lucky she was. Everyone said how good they looked together. Everyone thought she was living the dream relationship with the handsome, affable, wealthy, caring Cole Carr.

But she wasn't feeling it.

When she was around him, she wasn't a hundred percent relaxed. She suffered through his kisses. She listened to his declarations of love and wondered in a panic if there was something wrong with her. Why couldn't she feel it?

Cole was perfect! He looked good, smelled good, didn't smoke, drink, flirt with other women, and was a faithful Christian. He came from a normal loving family who liked her. She was best friends with his sister, Yara.

And yet, she didn't feel it. She was self-sabotaging. If she could make herself love him, she would.

She stared at the reminder on her desk: Lunch at the gallery at 2!

The gallery was Cole's business place. He had a gallery upstairs where he sold paintings, including some of his own and downstairs, he had a booming graphics and printing service.

Today was 'd' day. The day she was supposed to answer his proposal. They would have a catered lunch; they would eat on the back patio overlooking the gardens, and Cole would look at her in anticipation, expecting an answer, and she would…

Tiana closed her eyes tightly.

She couldn’t say yes. She couldn't marry a man for whom she had no feelings.

She would have to break up with him. It was going to cause shock waves in her family, with his family, and of course with Yara. Everybody expected her to say yes.

Yara had been online picking out dresses from last year. She was both the best friend and maid-of-honor and the sister of the groom. Her disappointment would probably drive a wedge in their twenty-year friendship. They had been friends since prep school.

Tiana couldn’t marry Cole Carr just because she didn’t want to upset the apple cart. This was her future. She didn’t want to waste a life and ultimately make both of them miserable. She needed to talk to someone about this.

It couldn’t be Elsa.

Elsa was doing some important presentation today to some client at the advertising firm where she worked. It was her first time doing a presentation alone. It was all she talked about for the past two weeks.

Giselle was out of it too. Way out. She was in a different time zone. It was Diamond League time. She was probably sleeping or something.

It would have to be Yara. But Yara was too close to the situation. She loved her brother blindly. Maybe she wouldn't see Tiana's point of view objectively.

Her phone rang while she lamented in her head. She saw that it was Yara. They usually met for lunch at Yum Yum Café at the Wiley Complex. Yara was a Cyber Security Specialist at Wiley Securities.

She must have forgotten that today was not their day.

The Wiley Complex was on her way to the gallery, so she could still stop by and have a face to face talk with her friend.

She grabbed her bag and headed out of the office before

answering.

“Hey.” Even to her ears she didn't sound as upbeat as she usually did.

“Hey T, I can’t go to Yum Yum today," Yara said regretfully. “I have a big client that was hacked so my boss wants all hands on deck for this. However, you can come eat with me in the executive dining room. Garett has a favor to ask of you. He wants a document translated. It’s in French, and it’s just one page. It’s a part of some investigation he is doing.”

Tiana grunted. “I can’t today. I have lunch with Cole.”

“Oh, cool.” Yara chuckled. “Boyfriend trumps best friend. I’ll tell Garrett that you won’t be available.”

“I want to run something by you,” Tiana got into the car, “before lunch with Cole.”

“Okaaay," Yara said, dragging out the okay.

“I’ll be there in ten minutes.” Tiana sighed.

“You okay?” Yara asked fearfully.

“I am good,” Tiana said, “it’s nothing for you to worry about. I just…”

“You are pregnant!” Yara squealed. “You succumbed to my brother’s charm, decided not to wait until your honeymoon, and now I am going to be an aunt.”

“No!” Tiana said appalled. She had never once been tempted to succumb to Cole’s charm as Yara had put it. Just another one of the troubling signs that something was wrong with their chemistry.

And she knew she was capable of succumbing. It wasn’t that she was better or holier or more exemplary than other young women. In high school, if James Dalton had once given her even the slightest signal, she would have…

“A girl can hope," Yara said in her ear. “I wouldn't mind a shotgun wedding. Get it over and done with.”

“Yara…” Tiana sighed, “maybe I shouldn’t stop by.”

"You should," Yara whispered. "You need to see my new department head. He looks just like Lamman Rucker except younger and darker. I love dark-skinned men with impossibly white teeth and pink lips."

"I am not interested, Tiana chuckled, "I thought you had your sights set on Dr. Ace Jackson.

"I am running out of ailments, and I swear the man is on to me," Yara muttered, "there are so many broad hints a girl can give. I am going to have to move on."

Tiana laughed out loud. "You are crazy."

****

Tiana drove to the Wiley complex and parked before Wiley Securities. As usual, she ran into a Wiley family member or two when she was there. Today it was her brother-in-law, Pete. He was in the lobby and on the phone when she saw him. He waved to her and ended the call quickly.

"Hey, Tiana. One moment."

"Pete," Tiana smiled, "how are you. How is it going?"

He grinned. "I know right, such a long time. Can you do me a teensy favor? It's not on the schedule, but I am in a tight spot."

He was referring to the babysitting arrangement that she and Elsa agreed to participate in while Giselle was away for the summer.

"Sure." Tiana nodded.

"Pick up Ethan from Liz for me this Thursday. I am going to be working out of town, and I won't be back until late. I will pick him up Friday morning."

"Sure." Tiana grimaced. "That would mean seeing Liz Morgan, but she could do that."

Pete looked at her hesitantly. "And I hate to do this to the schedule again, but I have a wedding to attend in Portland next Sunday. The bride is a long-time employee of my dad. She asked me to sing. So if you keep Ethan overnight that Sunday, I would be grateful."

"Sure." Tiana nodded. "No problem."

She loved babysitting her adorable nephew. It was Giselle's busiest time of year, so everybody chipped in with Ethan to help out Pete.

"I meant overnight," Pete clarified. "I am traveling with my parents and they won't be back until Monday."

"Sure." Tiana nodded. "I am free next Sunday, it's no big deal."

He paused. "Er…I…know you try to avoid Liz, but she is leaving to go back to the UK next week, and Shawn is having a goodbye party on that Sunday. She wants to do a photo shoot with all the kids and Liz."

Tiana made a face.

"Which means you have to take him," Pete said slowly as if she was hard of hearing. "You'll have to be at the party. I would've asked Elsa, but she won't be in Kingston that weekend."

"You owe me," Tiana grumbled. "You will owe me, big time."

"Thanks a bunch." Pete smiled. "You are an exemplary aunt, taking one for the team."

He grinned at Tiana and gave her a thumbs-up before hurrying away.

Tiana smirked.

She had been trying to avoid Lizette Morgan from the moment she had started working with the Wileys. Giselle and Pete teased her mercilessly about it. They were sure that Liz Morgan had no idea that she was the girl who had gotten her son fired from school, ruined his relationship and left him homeless.

Tiana was not so sure. She was convinced that James Dalton had a banner on his front porch that had her face and a negative red sign superimposed over it.

Yara exited the elevator before she could reach the receptionist desk. Her friend was a standout in any crowd. She was tall, leggy and slim with a smooth mocha-colored skin and the most exquisite fine features. She had the kind of face that looked good, whether she was bald or had hair.

She usually preferred her hair cut very close to her scalp, especially in the summer. And that's how she had it now.

People naturally assumed Yara was a model of some sort, but Yara had never even considered it. She was a tech geek, a security expert who loved to read mystery novels and solve cases. She also liked dabbling in investigative work even though that was not her division at Wiley Securities. She was naturally good at investigating.

They were friends since grade school, and tighter than glue and paper. Nobody quite got her like Yara did, not even her sisters Elsa or Giselle.

They greeted each other enthusiastically as if they didn't have lunch together every day.

"Wifey!" Yara squealed when she saw her.

"Wifey!" Tiana grinned back.

"I have just ten minutes to talk," Yara said regretfully. "What's the face to face emergency?"

"I er…" Tiana deflected, "I did something ridiculous today. I threw caution to the wind and entered a writing interview of sorts."

"I like when you say you throw caution to the wind." Yara's big brown eyes lit up. "I hope you get shortlisted."

"Thank you," Tiana said forlornly, "I found out afterward that the company was JD Productions."

"JD Productions?" Yara raised an eyebrow. "Never heard of them."

"Secrets of Love, Nemesis, and Clandestine." Tiana said, "all television series that you know and love."

"Ah," Yara nodded. "Cool."

"JD stands for James Dalton," Tiana said. "I looked it up."

"Oh, snap." Yara widened her eyes. "You are going to see him again.

"I may not be shortlisted." Tiana said, "and even if I were, one look at my name, and he is going to chuck me off the list."

"I don't know," Yara whispered, "I think James had a soft spot for you back in high school. Why else would he have put up with your stories for so long? If it were anybody else, they would have been called out, disciplined, shamed publicly. Your stories were hot and totally inappropriate, and you used to sign them, To Sir With Love. So corny…"

"I wasn't the only girl who pursued him," Tiana said uncomfortably.

"Girl, you were the only one who did it with single-minded determination. He was an obsession." Yara glanced at her, "I am happy that phase is over. You were relentless. Thank God you got over that. I think Cole had a softening effect on you when you decided to give him the time of day."

They got into the elevator. Tiana sighed. "About that."

Yara glanced at her sharply. "Don't say it, Tiana."

Tiana groaned. "I shouldn't be here. I should just go to lunch with Cole and tell him how I feel."

They reached Yara's floor. Yara led the way to her office and closed the door.

"You are breaking up with my brother?" She sat in her chair and stared at Tiana stonily across the desk.

Tiana sat down with a sigh. "I can't feel it, Yara. I tried. I tried for you, I tried for your parents and Toddy and Giselle and Elsa and all of our mutual friends. I gave it my best shot, but if I marry him, I will end up hurting both of us."

Yara grimaced. "But he loves you."

"I know." Tiana looked down at her hands, "but I don't love him."

"Because you've only ever loved one man." Yara shook her head, "why can't you just shake him out of your head and move on? What was it about James Dalton anyway? My brother is equally as handsome, and he is super smart and artistic, and he would jump through hoops for you. Do you know how many women would give their right arm to be with Cole?"

Tiana stared at Yara. "You are not going to have a meltdown over this are you?"

"No," Yara gritted out, "maybe you should see a therapist about your unrequited love for a man in your past who you never had a relationship with, never had any experiences with, who was out of your reach. I don't even know if you can call it love. Your therapist would have a field day with this conundrum."

Tiana sighed. "I don't think I have an unrequited love for James Dalton, but I've never felt the same way about anyone else. Maybe I burned it all out back then. How do you think Cole will take this?"

"Badly." Yara drummed her fingers on the table. "Terrible. He'll probably paint a couple of paintings of you disfigured."

"Uhh, I can't have disfigured paintings of me around the place," Tiana said half-jokingly. "So do you think I should marry him then to spare the world that eyesore?"

"Yes!" Yara nodded vigorously and then subsided in her chair. "I mean, I don't know. Don't hurt Cole. Don't break up with him yet. He is vulnerable, he loves you."

"You are angry at me," Tiana whispered. "I don't want you angry."

"Disappointed, not angry," Yara growled. "I had dreams of you being my sister by marriage and being your maid-of-honor and being an aunty and all of that jazz. You are ruining the fantasy."

"I think this job interview is divine intervention."

"You do?" Tiana asked. "Why?"

"You should meet James Dalton again as an adult," Yara drummed her fingers on the table, "with maturity comes perspective. You'll probably realize that he is not all that and what you had for him in high school was a fluke. You'll be released from your fantasy and then you'll see my brother for what he is, the best thing that ever happened to you."

"Okay." Tiana nodded.

"And even if you are not shortlisted," Yara leaned over the desk, "you should go see him. Talk to him. Set yourself free."

"No, I wouldn't do that." Tiana gasped. "I wouldn't just go and see him like that. He would probably call the police."

"No, he wouldn't," Yara snorted. "You remember that picture you gave him of yourself on your birthday."

"Yes," Tiana smirked, "I signed it to sir with love, and he gave it back to me."

"He didn't just give it back," Yara drummed her fingers on the desk, "didn't he write something on the back?"

"Yes," Tiana nodded, "he wrote right Pryce wrong time. What do you think that means?"

"It's obvious he was saying, 'Yeah right, Tiana Pryce. This is the wrong time to be messing with me.'" Yara mused, "You have to clear this man out of your system. You loved and obsessed over somebody who didn't even like you."

"Rub it in thick, why don't you?" Tiana growled. "I'll take

your advice."

"I hope to God, he has gotten uglier and is married and has grown a beer belly and has cigarette stained teeth and smells like a pig."

Tiana chuckled. "I doubt that."

"One can hope," Yara said faintly.

Tiana got a message on her phone at the same time. She looked at the text. It was from Cole. Babe, running late, can we take a raincheck on lunch?

Sure, she typed back.

She looked at Yara. "Well, it seems as if I am not going to break up with Cole today."

"Thank you, God," Yara said feelingly. "Promise me you will keep an open mind. You'll see James before, and then you decide."

Tiana twisted her lips. "I don't know…"

"Just promise," Yara insisted, "no breaking up with Cole until you are sure you are not just hanging on to a dream."

"Okay," Tiana said uncertainly. "I promise."

"Make sure you come to choir practice." Yara grinned, "I heard tonight is going to be special."

"Most definitely will be there." Tiana got up. "See you later."

Chapter Three

Choir practice was her favorite thing to do on Friday evenings. Tiana thought as she drove into the church parking lot. Since Cole had joined the choir, it had begun to pall a bit for her. She was conflicted over him, and their relationship and she couldn't quite escape into the songs as before.

She was twenty minutes early. She sat in her car and closed her eyes, now things would have been perfect if she had the same kind of heady emotions directed toward Cole that she had for James Dalton.

She allowed herself, just for a moment, to indulge in the past. She didn't do that much these days because she usually cringed when she thought about it.

Six years ago…

"How was your Christmas holiday with your big sister?" Yara asked. They had just gotten back from the holidays, one of the worst ones to date. For the first time, she and her sisters had split up at the end of the year. Giselle had done training camp; Elsa had gone to Miami to spend time with their aunt Sharla, and she had gotten the short straw. She had been forced by Toddy and a flip of a coin to go to Caroline's for the Christmas. Caroline was her eldest sister.

After ignoring them for many years, Caroline had suddenly and inexplicably decided that she wanted them with her for the holiday.

"She is lonely," Toddy said sternly, "it's only natural. For many years she has been all about her career. She is now semi-retired and trying to make amends."

"But why me?" Tiana whined.

"Because you said heads." Toddy grinned, "the triplet that says heads goes to Caroline, tails goes to Sharla."

"Hello," Yara snapped her fingers in front of Tiana's face, "it couldn't have been that bad."

"It wasn't." Tiana sighed. "It was New York. It could have been nice if I had gone with family I could relate to, but Caroline is different. She's rich and old with an impeccable apartment that is obviously posh and speaks so proper. She was always correcting everything I said. And we went to one endless dinner party after another with a lot of judges and law professors and fellow old people who thought I was an oddity."

Yara chuckled.

"One of them even hit on me. He looks like he has nine toes in a coffin."

Yara laughed out loud. "Describe him."

"Pale, wrinkly, white with dentures that are obviously too big for his mouth. He kept saying how exotic looking I was and kept asking why Caroline didn't tell him she had a lovely Latina granddaughter. I said Sir, I am not Latina. I am black, and I am Caroline's younger sister from my father's second marriage. I had to shout because he was hard of hearing.

And then he looked at me and said, "I can't marry you, child. My wife is still alive!"

"When Caroline heard that she started giggling. That's the only human crack I saw in her armor.

"She said the old man was some supreme court judge or the other, she couldn't stop cracking up about it."

"And that, my dear, Yara," Tiana imitated Caroline's accent, "was the extent of the jollity for my holiday."

Yara shook her head. "A supreme court judge, huh? Those are lofty circles your sister travels in."

"Yep." Tiana nodded. "She is an appeals court justice and was shortlisted for the supreme court by some president or the other, and that was a huge deal. I acted sufficiently impressed, but I had no idea what she was going on about until I read a Tom Clancy novel."

Yara looked at her wide-eyed. "Are you serious now?"

"Yes," Tiana nodded, "the story was about this judge who was on trial for a crime…"

Yara started laughing.

"You only know about the law system because both your parents are lawyers." Tiana grimaced. "I had no clue."

"And my brother was studying to be a lawyer." Yara chuckled, "but he quit, he said he wants to do art and graphic design. My parents haven't quite recovered. He is still in Canada doing a totally different course now."

"At least they'll get all the shock out of their system when you tell them you want to be an investigator." Tiana chuckled, "an adult Nancy Drew."

"I already told them." Yara shrugged. "They didn't care. They want me to do whatever I want to do."

Tiana nodded. "I think Toddy wants me to join his

advertising business."

"But your sole ambition is to be James Dalton's groupie." Yara sighed. "You have no other talents or desires."

"Speaking of the devil." Yara straightened up in her seat when James Dalton stepped into the classroom but was stopped by a student who was having a whispered conversation with him. "The man just keeps on getting better looking over the years. He looks darker today, yum dot com."

Tiana turned to the front of the class and stared at him too. Yara was right. He was darker, which brought out his green eyes, which was further enhanced by his green shirt.

"I say he was at the beach all holiday," Yara murmured. "Maybe Cancun or some other exotic destination, half-naked with a bevy of girls crawling all over him."

"He is a teacher; how could he afford that?" Tiana whispered. "I think he was somewhere in Jamaica at a family members house, and he went surfing or just lazed away the days, alone and lonely pining for me."

"Nah, he moonlights as a model," Yara smiled, "and he is just doing the teaching thing until he gets his big break."

"He doesn't strike me as the model type," Tiana whispered, "he is too, I don't know, serious."

"Intellectual." Yara supplied. "Strict. Severe."

"And he doesn't smile," Tiana muttered, "or maybe he is only that way with me. He smiles with other students."

"Maybe if you didn't insist on signing all of your classwork with, to sir with love, or stalked him around campus or drooled at the sight of him, he wouldn't be so standoffish." Yara glared at her. "You are giving me a bad rep by association."

"Sorry," Tiana shrugged, "my new year's resolution will be to find my dignity around James Dalton."

"Good." Yara nodded.

"Right after I kiss him," Tiana said dreamily, "that's

another resolution. I have to kiss him this year. It's my final year in high school, my final class with him. I want him to remember me."

"You are crazy," Yara groaned, "hopeless."

"I have to get it out of my system. I'll be eighteen in a few days, and he is the one that I want my first kiss with, my first everything with. We can have a relationship when I start university this year. He won't be my teacher anymore."

"He doesn't want you, girl." Yara laughed. "He is engaged to be married; didn't he tell you that? You are just a stalker, and when you think about it, he is half afraid of you. Open up your eyes T, he barely makes eye contact with you in class. He warned you about your erotic essays and threatened to set the guidance counselor on you if you continue."

"He feels it too," Tiana said defiantly. "He is into me. This thing that we have between us cannot be one-sided, we are drawn to each other. He is just better at hiding it because he is my teacher, and a relationship between us would be taboo. If he weren't my teacher, we would be together now. He is just four years older than I am. That's nothing."

"Wrong, everything is wrong with the whole mad scenario you have going on in your head," Yara grumbled. "You are drinking your own mad Kool-Aid."

"I am going to arrange for the kiss," Tiana said determinedly, "you can come and document it for posterity. You'll see how into me he is."

"Fine. Yara chuckled. "If your mouth ever touches James Dalton's this year, I will not only document it, I will never again call you mad."

"It's a deal." Tiana grinned.

****

“You were so far away, Tiana," Susie said near her ears. “Were you in a trance?”

“Something like that.” Tiana looked at Susie. “Is it time for rehearsal yet?”

“No,” Susie muttered, “I am not even sure I can sing this evening; my voice is tired, but I had to come, tonight is special.”

“Why?” Tiana asked. “Yara said it was special too.”

“Every choir practice is special,” Susie said sheepishly. “The male section of the choir this year is something else. It’s as if Dillon got all the scrumptious men in the church and plonked them into one place.”

Tiana laughed. “And it doesn’t help that the updated black and gold choir robes look so good on them.”

“Seriously,” Susie whispered as they approached the church steps, “is Dillon choosing the choir based on looks, you have the Jackson brothers— Ace, Deuce, Trey, then the Wiley’s —Peter and Case. Not to mention Cole Carr—taken by you but still counts.

Susie paused for a breath. “Then there is Chad, Chuck, Lester…I could go on, not one ugly one. This is a blessed and highly favored church. The day I moved my membership here was a day blessed of God.”

Tiana chuckled. “Who is your favorite?”

“Out of the singles?” Susan grinned. “I would have said Cole, but you have him, girl. That man is into you. If I could have a man that is so dedicated to me, I wouldn't want anything else. I would praise God every day, I would have married him already.”

Tiana laughed.

It was a good-looking choir. Susie was not exaggerating, and they had the famous Case Wiley who occasionally showed up to sing with them when he was in Jamaica. They had even done backing vocals on his Dove winner, Case, and God.

Dillon liked to tell the church and whoever wanted to listen that they were an award-winning choir.

They got started later than usual, most of them were professionals or ran their own businesses. They were busy people. Tonight forty of them showed up which meant that most of them were there.

She saw when Cole slipped in when they were warming up. He flashed her a smile and blew her a kiss. She smiled back at him and then turned away uncomfortably, why did he have to be so over the top?

"Okay, let's get cracking," Dillon said. "Let's have some fun."

The choir knew what that meant. Dillon had them practicing —Turn, Turn Turn, by the Byrds which was based on the third chapter of Ecclesiastes. They had their specific parts and really enjoyed belting it out.

To everything turn, turn, turn
There is a season turn, turn, turn
And a time to every purpose
Under Heaven

A time of love, a time of hate
A time of war, a time of peace
A time you may embrace
And now is the time, Tiana will you marry me?

"Huh?" Tiana was so into the song she didn't realize that they had changed the words. Everybody was looking at her.

Brad, who was on the drums and Greg, who was on the piano, started it again. They sang it a second time.

Cole was at the front of the choir; he had made his way over to the soprano section where she was, and he was on one knee a ring box in his hand.

The choir paused. Greg was playing softly, everybody waited for her to respond.

Tiana squealed in her head. No!! No!!! Oh, God, no!!

But everybody was there and looking at her so excited. They had planned this!

"Yes!" She said out loud.

Cole got up, put the ring on her finger, they kissed while the choir started the song again.

She was panicking on the inside.

Chapter Four

James stepped into the Morgan Great House entryway feeling as if he had stepped back in time. Even his uncle Reginald Morgan looked as if he belonged in the eighteenth century with tailcoat and long jacket, his silk top hat perched on his head.

He looked exactly like the first Reginald Morgan whose portrait was prominently displayed in the grand hall, narrow face, dirty blond hair and green eyes.

Light from realistic-looking candles was blazing throughout the place.

"Holy smokes," Traci whispered beside him. "It's an honest to goodness great house. My ancestors would die again in shock if they knew I was staying with the massa in the big house."

James chuckled. Traci was as usual dramatic to a fault. "The first Reginald Morgan was biracial. His mother was a slave woman. He only passed as white."

"Scandalous." Traci grinned. "I'll feel more at home then."

Reginald laughed. "Our family has a torrid and entertaining history. Welcome nephew, I was anticipating you and your crew to be here much earlier than this."

"The flight was delayed. There is no crew," James indicated to Traci his assistant and Jose, his writer colleague, "just us. We need to write your story first, make it television worthy before we bring in the others."

"Oh, I know." Reginald rubbed his hands together. "I am looking forward to the whole process. I am beside myself with excitement."

James smiled; his uncle's excitement was infectious. "I didn't know you were putting us up in the big house."

"Yes, I am. The coach house is being renovated; it's taking painstakingly long, but it should be ready for filming, the bookkeeper's house is where I am staying. Your crew and the other writers can stay in the cottages. I made sure a dozen were available for them. Is that too little?"

"It's too much for now." James ran his hand over his face. "I am just going to crash; we just finished the second season of Unrequited. We had a couple of sleepless nights."

"Can I get a preview?" Reginald asked, "I love that show."

"Of course," James smiled back, "anything for my main investor."

Traci had wandered off to explore the vast great house hall. Jose had joined her; they were so taken up with the antiques that they had forgotten that they were tired.

"Is this original?" Jose asked reverently, staring at the grand piano.

"Yes, it is." Reginald turned to him. "Every furniture in this house is original. When it was built in the late 1700s by the first Morgan, he decided to get quality pieces. That piano still has the same powerful, rich tones because of its stringing."

"I would like to give it a try," Jose said reverently.

"He is a history professor, avid musician, and prolific author, and he is on sabbatical," James said to Reginald. "Perfect fit for this miniseries."

"I'd say." Reginald smiled broadly. "You can play the piano anytime you wish, Jose. I'll even give you a special tour tomorrow so that we can discuss the history of the time. I am something of a history aficionado myself, my sons and nephew are quite bored with me now and zone out when I get started. I am always on the lookout for fellow history lovers."

"But for now, I am sure you are all tired. I'll have Beatrice show you to your quarters. If you would like anything at all, Beatrice is here to see to your comfort."

Beatrice glided into the great hall as if on cue.

"Welcome to Jamaica, Miss Traci, Mr. Jose, and Mr. Handsome. Beatrice beamed at him, "I have not seen your pretty face in ages. You should come home more often."

James grinned. "Thank you, Beatrice. I missed seeing your pretty face too."

Reginald laughed. "James, sleep well. You can update me tomorrow, until then I remain anxious to hear what is next."

"I know, I will give you a thorough briefing tomorrow."

"Very well," Reginald said in a posh British accent that he had not quite managed to lose even after spending most of the last twenty years in the tropics.

"I will see you in the morning. I anticipated that the library will be your new office. It is well equipped with all the necessary technological gadgets. We even have Wi-Fi, not very period-specific, but one has to join the current world sometimes. I will see you there mid-morning."

"Come along, folks." Beatrice smiled, "Mr. Jose and Miss

Traci, you are in the west wing."

They headed up the wide staircase behind Beatrice's round figure. She wore a long brown dress and matching head wrap that would not be out of place in the eighteenth century. James had given up guessing Beatrice's age. She had unlined coffee-colored skin which looked perpetually cool and line free. She could be anywhere from fifty to seventy.

She turned around and smiled at Traci and Jose. "You will love it here."

She quickly showed Traci and Jose to their separate rooms. James followed them, pulling his suitcase wearily. In the morning he would take his time to walk around the house.

"Wow, this is more spacious than I thought it would be." Traci exclaimed, "and it's cool. Why is it cool? It was hot when we stepped out of the airport."

"We are on top of a hill," Beatrice said, "it doesn't get hot up here. You will have a good night. Our guests always wake up feeling refreshed. There is something about this spot, it is God blessed."

She turned to James and beamed; her round face creased in a smile. "Sir Reginald wanted you in the east wing suite."

James grinned. "That's fancy."

Beatrice laughed. "He wants you comfortable and creative. Come this way."

James followed her. "He is buttering me up. From I was a little boy I can remember him wanting someone to do a series about the Morgans."

"Ahem," Beatrice cleared her throat, "I would like to officially try to butter you up too. I want a part in the movie. I can be an extra. Sir Reg, already has us wearing period costumes I'll fit right in."

"It's not a movie," James said when Beatrice opened the suite and stepped aside. "It is a mini-series. Maybe ten or twelve episodes."

Beatrice grinned. "Good. I can appear in more than one episode then?"

"Sure." James grinned. "I'll see what I can do."

"And don't cut me out of the final takes either." Beatrice wagged a finger at him. "My friend Octavia thought she was going to be in a movie, and they cut out her scene."

"I won't cut you out." James smiled.

"Good, Beatrice beamed and then changed the subject, her face getting serious. "You know Krista is here for the summer?"

James went still. "Really?"

"Yes, summer holiday. She heard you were coming, and she wants to ask for your forgiveness. You two ended so abruptly."

"She accused me of having an affair with my student." James frowned. "She didn't listen to my side of the story. She was the one who ended it abruptly. I phoned her several times to talk to me and work it out. I even showed up at her door, and she slammed the door in my face."

"I know," Beatrice said soothingly. "But time has passed now. Forgive her."

"I did." James shrugged. "A long time ago. I got over Krista. I thought she would have been married by now."

"She married a couple months after her relationship with you ended." Beatrice grimaced. "It never worked out. The guy was abusive."

"She left me for an abuser." James shook his head. "Well, I guess that's life."

Beatrice sighed. "Can you do me a favor, James?"

"What?" James asked harshly. He didn't mean to snap at Beatrice, but it stung a little that Krista had gotten married so soon after scraping him out of her life.

"Can you give her a place on your writing team?" Beatrice asked in a rush. "You know she is a good writer. Can you forgive her enough to give her a chance?"

"Beatrice, the advocate." James twisted his lips. He knew Krista was a good writer, they had attended the same classes at university. She had graduated magna cum laude and moved on to a masters in English while he had worked as a teacher.

She would be the perfect fit for the current project, she grew up right here. She knew the history of the Morgans more than she knew her own family history.

He was surprised that Beatrice was the one who was asking him to hire Krista. Krista was Sir Reggie's ward. He had taken care of her financially for most of her life. If she had appealed to Reggie, he would not have hesitated to tell James that she should be included. This independent route was confusing him.

"You loved her once." Beatrice urged him, still doing her best to plead Krista's case. "I still remember when you two were children, running around here like two peas in a pod. It had always been Krista for you. You told me when you were five that you would marry her, remember?"

James sighed. The appeal to his childhood with Krista had the desired effect. He would always have a soft spot for her. She had been his first girlfriend. His first love. But he had lived a lot of life since Krista.

"Let me sleep on it, huh. I'll give you my answer tomorrow."

"Thank you." Beatrice nodded. "You are a good man, James, you always were. Enjoy your stay here. I drew you a bath, the water is warm. If you need anything at all, I am on call twenty-four hours. I am at the staff quarters at the back. I'll just run over."

James nodded. "Thank you, Beatrice."

"No problem." Beatrice shut the door, and he sank down in the nearest chair. It was not comfortable though. He looked up at the tray ceiling and at the intricate painting of cherubim and grapes and gold curlicues.

Every detail in the sitting room looked like he was still in the early 1800s. Even the electric light fixtures looked like relics of the past.

The sitting room was lit with flickering electric candles with realistic wax pooling at the sides. It looked so much like the real thing that James leaned over the one closest to him to make sure that it wasn't.

The sitting room was decorated to reflect the Georgian styles of Europe and was in incredibly good shape. The floors were made of mahogany, polished to perfection by the dedicated staff. Upstairs had a wraparound veranda just like downstairs and jalousies and sash windows instead of solid wall, it made the place perpetually airy and cool.

Ironically, he had never stayed in the great house. That privilege was reserved for high paying guests who wanted a great house experience. Sir Reggie had turned the place into a high-end bed and breakfast after his father, Fitzgerald Morgan, had gifted it to him.

When James visited Morgan Great House as an adult, he had always stayed with Sir Reggie in a less palatial abode some distance away. That house was also Georgian in design had been the bookkeeper's residence.

The property also had a church which was almost as old as the great house and was incredibly well preserved, and an old hospital that was now used as storage.

He grew up in the great house village five miles away, to the east, near the sea. In the 1800s that village was the slave quarters for the great house. It had been an extensive community then as it was now. Most of the people who lived in the village were employed by his paternal uncle.

His grandfather had been a cook in the main house. He died when James was seven. His grandmother had lived in the village and ran a haberdashery.

His grandmother died of a heart attack in her sleep when he was twelve. His mother was forced to take him to live with her in England after that because his father had been deployed by the US Army to a secret mission and couldn't be reach in time.

James winced. He didn't want to be sitting in the living room thinking about his childhood. He usually didn't like to think of that time in his life when his mother brought him, the child of an affair with her Jamaican boyfriend, to live with her husband and girls. He might as well have been transplanted among aliens.

It was mutual dislike from the get-go. He had missed his nonna fiercely.

And there he was transplanted among strangers who didn't like him much. His three older sisters hated him on sight, and his stepfather called him that thing.

That's why he got lost in books as a coping mechanism. And maybe that was why he overused his imagination. He was always imagining the type of family that he wished he had and not the one he ended up getting.

That is why when he came back to Jamaica to attend college and met up with Krista at Mount Faith, he was so quick to embrace her. She had represented home. A piece of it that he had thought he lost. He had fancied himself in love.

And he had carried that feeling with him until he had met Tiana Pryce.

Tiana Pryce had made him question everything. She had gotten under his skin. She had made him question his own decency and sense of morality.

He clamped down on that chain of thought. He needed a bath, maybe that would clear his mind. He headed for the en suite bathroom. It still had a claw foot tub that managed to look new and ancient at the same time, he could see the steam wafting up from the water. Someone had also put Fabiola petals in there.

Beatrice was giving him the royal treatment.

He stripped his clothes and tested the water before he stepped into the tub. It was the perfect temperature, and it smelled so good. He sank down in the tub with a groan of pleasure on his lips. This would do the trick.

He was relaxing. He closed his eyes, and Tiana Pryce's face imposed itself on the back of his eyelids. He opened them quickly again. Why was he thinking about her now?

He had thought about her off and on for years, especially in the earlier years but he had moved on and drawn a line under the whole Tiana situation. He closed his eyes and leaned back in the tub.

Chapter Five

September, eight years ago

James entered the classroom and looked around. It was his first day as a teacher in a high school and he felt like a fish out of water. He had done an English degree at the prestigious Mount Faith university and had no idea what he was going to do after the degree. He had always wanted to be a playwright and had put on quite a few community productions when he was at university, but something had to pay the bills and teaching would have to do in the short term.

It wasn't hard to get the job at Bellfield. His uncle was a benefactor to the school. All it took was one phone call, and he was in. There had actually been a vacancy to teach the upper classes, to prepare them for the external exams. The curriculum was not that bad, and unconventional learning methods were encouraged by the principal. The classes were small enough to meet each individual student's learning needs.

His current class had only fifteen students. It was his first encounter with a privately-run high school where the richest of the rich sent their offspring. He looked around at the overprivileged bunch, and then his eyes met hers.

He didn't know her name yet, he didn't know which rich parent she belonged to, but he knew without anyone spelling it out to him that she would be trouble.

One look and he felt spellbound. He dragged his eyes from her, resenting the effect she had on him.

She was pretty, and she knew it.

She continued staring at him as if she were assessing whether to give him the time of day. He should find it ludicrous; he was her teacher, not some potential suitor, but somehow, he couldn't drum up the disdain he should be feeling at the preposterous situation.

Mrs. Munroe, the principal's voice, rang in his head, they had met in her office just a few minutes before. Mrs. Munroe had looked formidable with her over-plucked eyebrows and steely grey eyes.

"We have zero tolerance for teacher and student hookups. It was a problem here before I came on staff, but I nipped it in the bud.

"Some of the girls in our upper classes are sixteen years and over, some of them are working people, we have a few models, some app developers, a television hostess with a huge social media following."

She paused to take a breath, steepling her fingers under her chin. "We have an actress, a sports star or two, a few of them own businesses, one girl just got the patent for some invention or the other. Obviously, we are not dealing with the normal student at this school. Some of them are heirs and heiresses to large fortunes. Some of them have the attitude that school is just a formality. It is easy to forget that they are students."

"Wow," James muttered, "apparently high school is not what it used to be in my days."

"This high school is atypical." Mrs. Munroe pushed up her glasses on her nose. "We need you in the upper classes, those are the sixteen to eighteen-year-olds.

"You are a good-looking male teacher. It will be mayhem here when they first see you. Hopefully, the euphoria will peter out. Until then, you'll need to be careful. And I say this to all my male teachers, of course, these days I have to say the same thing to the females too. This world is not the same as when I was a young teacher, I'll tell you that."

James widened his eyes. "You make this sound dangerous."

Mrs. Munroe leaned back in her chair. "We have had quite a few incidents with male teachers, and female teachers as well, having closer than usual relationships with students. We learn from them. I am being realistic Mr. Dalton. These girls do not act like children, even the lower grades. You are a little older than some of them. Are you capable of handling the mob?"

"Yes." James had looked at Mrs. Munroe bemusedly. Surely, she wasn't serious. It could not be that bad.

"They'll send you underwear in packages. Pay for you to go away with them to hotels for dirty weekends. Just remember you are in authority here."

James nodded.

"Zero fraternizing." She emphasized again. "No texting, phone calls, after school chats in locked offices, no encouragement of friendships. No casual first-name references. You have to be firm with them, or you are out of here. We are a private school with many powerful benefactors, the slightest whiff of impropriety and you are gone."

James nodded again briskly. He wondered if she would be impressed if he told her that he had a fiancée who was finishing up her master's degree. He had no desire for high school girls with too much money and not enough sense.

"Don't cross the line, Mr. Dalton," Mrs. Munroe said unsmilingly. "Remember that."

He didn't need her to tell him twice.

He was keeping this job. No student was going to derail him.

****

He looked down at the fifteen names on the digital register. Eleven of them were girls. His eyes ran down the list, and he saw the name, Tiana. He instinctively knew it was her. Tiana meant princess. She had that look about her. She was probably a spoiled princess too. She got everything she wanted without having to lift a finger.

"Tiana," he said out loud.

She waved her hand lazily, a small smile playing around her lips. "Here I am."

He hurriedly looked back at the register and called another name.

He clicked on each name, not going in any particular order because he had already given in to the weak impulse to call her name first.

Strike one against him.

He didn't allow himself to get many strikes after that. Mrs. Munroe had been right. The girls were relentless.

"You need a scar." One of his colleagues said to him jokingly, "but then again, a scar on your face would probably have them thinking you are mysterious and dangerous."

As time went by, he got used to the fawning attention. They eventually settled down; he became a regular face around campus. No longer a shiny newcomer.

But one student stood out for him. Tiana Pryce.

He couldn't avoid her. She wrote him long essays which should have a PG warning on them. She was imaginative and creative, but he had to tell her several times to tone it down.

He was one year into his job at Bellfield when Krista came over his apartment to spend the weekend with him. He was marking papers.

And she offered to help. Unfortunately, she happened upon one of Tiana's spicy essays that read like a bodice ripper on steroids, it starred her favorite male character, Wames Walton, who looked just like him. It didn't take a genius to figure out that he was the star of Tiana's imagination. And of course, she had attached a suggestive picture of herself on the paper. That was a new thing.

Krista looked at the picture and then at him in shock. "This girl, you should report her."

"It's harmless," he had said lazily. "The school encourages creativity; she has a budding career as a writer, don't you think?"

"No!" Krista had yelled. "This is not proper. You need to tell her to stop it. Is this picture of her harmless too?"

Krista had ripped up the essay and flung the picture into the farthest corner of the room. "Tell her to do another one that is age-appropriate and to stay in her own lane."

James had never seen Krista so mad.

"Why are you so triggered by this?" He had asked bewildered, "she is just a student, a girl you have never even met."

"But I know her type. Pretty, entitled, rich girl. She looks like a spoiled little prima donna. No, she is not just a student." Krista growled. "You like her little erotic essays. You like her!"

James had stared at Krista, rigid with shock.

"Deny it James." Krista had looked at him stricken.

"I don't understand where this is coming from."

"You talk in your sleep. You call her name in your sleep. Are you having an affair with her?"

"No!" James frowned. "I can't be held responsible for what my subconscious does when I am sleeping. You heard me say Tiana Pryce in my sleep?"

"No, just Tiana or Princess." Krista blinked rapidly. "I looked her up on social media, she's pretty. Just admit you have the hots for her and be honest. Then we can deal with it."

James looked cornered. "No, I will not admit that. Why are you looking her up on social media anyway?"

"We have the same surname." Krista barked, "and as I discovered the same eyes. You know I am trying to find my family. I was curious."

"This is much ado about nothing," James said dismissively.

"I don't think so," Krista said, "since you started teaching at Bellfield something changed with us. Now, I know why. It's this Tiana girl. Nip this in the bud, James, or I will."

He opened his mouth to protest and then closed it when he saw Krista's thunderous face.

"Okay," he said in defeat, "I'll tell her forcefully to back off with the essays. I don't have the hots for her. I am immune to my students."

Krista didn't look convinced.

****

He spoke to Tiana about her essays, and she toned them down somewhat. On her seventeenth birthday she wrote him a long heartfelt letter for which Krista would probably strangle him if she saw it.

He didn't want anyone to see that letter. It was filled with declarations of love and devotion, and she ended it with the line, I want you to be first, my last my only. I love you James.

It touched a chord within him. He could imagine her saying it, and it disturbed him. He didn't want to be affected, and he was mad at himself for feeling anything and mad at Tiana for letting him feel. He decided that for his peace of mind, he would have to be harsh with her. It was the only way. She had a few more years of growing up to do, and he was going to get married in the following year.

He decided to nip things in the bud after class on a Wednesday.

Tiana could you stay behind, please. "I want to discuss this essay. He held it up. But it wasn't the essay he was concerned about; it was her letter."

The rest of the class giggled.

"She's in trouble," one girl murmured. "I knew it was too hot for school."

Tiana looked at him guiltily all through class. She reluctantly walked over to him when everyone filed out and sat in the chair across from his desk, a look of defeat on her face.

It was the first time he was actually looking at her close up. Her eyelashes were longer than he had originally thought. The mole under her left eye was not a made up beauty mark, it was real. Her whiskey-colored eyes were even more interesting close-up.

She was not merely pretty, or girl next door cute, she was a beauty.

He could also see the adoration in her eyes as she gazed at him. He watched as she licked her lips nervously.

And suddenly he felt like doing the same. He had to put a stop to this, never in his life had he felt this way. He couldn't feel this way. She was his student. It would be an unequal relationship. He had a duty to protect her from herself and her obvious infatuation.

He inhaled raggedly; he was going to have to be cruel to be kind.

"Tiana, you cannot continue to send me pictures," he handed her back the picture she had stapled to her essay, "and you cannot write me letters like this."

He picked up the note that he had saved in his teacher's diary and read out loud to her, "I want you James. I need you like I have never needed anyone before. I am seventeen now a year past the age of consent. Let's get together."

She hung her head lower.

"If you write me anything like this again, I am taking it to the school guidance counselor."

Tiana looked up at him; her eyes flashing. "No!"

"I will. You obviously need an intervention," James said dispassionately. "I think your parents should be involved too."

"I don't have any parents." Tiana smirked at him. "Why are you doing this? I'll be discrete if we have an affair. I'll not tell anyone. Not even my sisters."

"Keep your voice down." James sat up, straighter in his chair.

"Tiana, we cannot have a relationship. I am your teacher. I am flattered that you are interested in me, but I am not interested in you. You are a girl who is undergoing a particularly virulent form of infatuation, if your essays are anything to go by. Please stop writing me letters and suggestive essays. If you write another, I am going to report it."

"But why?" Tiana looked at him, her long lashes fluttering. "Why can't you like me back? What's wrong with me? Didn't you hear I am past the age of consent? I want this. I love you. There are a million and one boys that like me. Even some of my brothers' friends like me, and they are way older than you."

James inhaled. "I am in a position of authority over you. If we had any kind of relationship, it would be wrong professionally. Besides, I have a fiancée."

He had dragged Krista out of his hat like a magician. "I love her, I should not be explaining myself to an out of control teenage girl. Either stop writing me these explicit letters, or I'll report it. This is your last chance. Teenage girls are more trouble than they are worth."

He had gotten up and left her in the classroom. He had glanced back at her to see what she was doing; she had her head down on the desk, quietly sobbing.

He had felt a shred of sympathy, but he had to harden his heart.

Unfortunately, he hadn't quite had his guard up when Tiana had sent him a note a few weeks before her summer exam and asked him to meet her in his office, he had thought she had settled down, she had stopped stalking him, and her essays had become quite tame and age-appropriate.

He had shared an office with two other staff members that year. The teachers who taught the pre-university students had some semi-privacy.

He had walked into the office, and Tiana was sitting waiting for him, and once more, he had remarked in his head how beautiful she was. She turned her amber eyes to him, and he found himself wondering not for the first time if she had on mascara. They were thick and distinctive like little fans.

"Mr. Dalton." She swallowed and then looked down at her hands.

"Yes, Tiana." His voice wasn't as steady as it should be. He didn't know what it was about her; she had a drugging effect on his senses.

He shouldn't be in an office with her alone. He knew that, and he was feeling slightly panicked about it. Maybe that was why he wasn't as quick to react when Tiana got up and threw herself at him, reaching up to put her hands around his neck and to place her soft, pillow soft lips on his.

The feel of her lips on his had shocked him rigid and rendered him unable to move for a split second while his body and all his senses came alive.

He had almost pulled her in and crushed her to him, and then good sense had prevailed, and he had pushed her away belatedly.

The only kiss that never really happened that had been the most memorable in his life.

****

James jolted out of his reverie when the water turned colder than was comfortable. He dragged himself out of the tub, feeling like a million years old. He wondered where Tiana was now. She would be what, twenty-four? She was probably living a life of leisure as some rich man's wife, or maybe she was modeling or just being a party girl. She had probably gotten around the block a few times with too many infatuations to count. With her looks, she probably caught men and then crushed them when she was tired of them.

He sighed. Why did the thought of that make him flinch? A part of him had always wanted to play the what-if game with Tiana Pryce.

Maybe he should look her up? Find out what she was up to. Maybe she wasn't even in Jamaica. He wouldn't do anything about the information, it would just be to assuage his curiosity.

He slid into bed and closed his eyes. At least he should be honest to himself in the darkest hour of the night in his uncle's eighteenth-century bed, he was more than a little curious about Tiana Pryce. At the back of his mind he had always liked her a little more than he should.

Chapter Six

James took a deep panting breath. Obviously, treadmills and fancy machines could not compensate for the real deal. It was early morning. He had gotten up a little before dawn while it was still dark out and took his daily run around the bicycle trail, part of which was uphill.

His uncle had added the trail years ago when he had taken up cycling for exercise. There was even a loaded bicycle rack beside the old bookkeeper's office. He had preferred to run instead of cycle.

He ran down to the village, he passed his former home where he had lived with his grandmother. He stopped and looked over at the stone cottage, someone else was living there now. The yard looked well-kept and neat. His grandmother's vegetable garden was obviously striving.

They had changed the windows to one of those modern ones with the mosquito mesh. He inhaled raggedly. He still missed his nonna. He probably would miss her forever. She had been Mrs. Nora James Dalton. He had her name. He inherited her personality and her looks. That was where his father got it from and he looked just like his dad, just a lighter version with green eyes.

He imagined himself running across the small lawn to tell his grandmother about his day at school. She always seemed to be so interested. He had never felt as comfortable with a person like he had been with his nonna. It had made his father jealous.

He grinned now, Milo Dalton had migrated to the States when he was just eighteen, but he returned every summer for a week or two to stay with his mother.

The summer when Milo was twenty, he met Lizzette Morgan Moore, bored housewife and mother to three little girls. She was sister to the Greathouse owner, Reginald Morgan, and on the forbidden list of women to mess with. Milo did not respect that rule, and neither did Lizzette.

They fell into an affair that resulted in him being conceived.

His mother had a choice of abandoning her marriage or leave him with Milo and move on with her marriage after her husband found out.

She had chosen her family in the UK and given him to Milo, who in turn had given him to his nonna, and they were fine.

Until they were not.

He made a face. His mother should have let him stay in Jamaica with his uncle Reggie and cousins at the great house. He would have had a much better time in his early teens. Except that Reggie had been going through his own marital problems at the time.

He snapped out of his reverie when the neighbor's door opened.

It was Krista Pryce. He would recognize her profile

anywhere. She was cute as ever, with a killer shape that had him drooling over her when he was in university. She was well proportioned, buxom, voluptuous. The kind of woman that turned heads, and she knew it. She was dressed in a blue tracksuit that highlighted all of her curves; a matching headband was around her thick curly hair.

It was much longer than before, reaching her way past her shoulders. He was the one to cut it when she had decided that she didn't want chemicals in her hair again. The short hair had suited her, bringing out her cheekbones, highlighting her amber eyes. The long hair looked good on her as well. Krista had the type of face that worked with any hairstyle.

"Hey." She grinned at him. "My aunt said you were finally here. You are all Sir Reggie talks about these days."

"Hey," James nodded. He walked close to her and smiled, "you are a sight for sore eyes."

"You too." Krista frowned. "You look so much like your father. How is that possible?"

"Thank you." James grinned. "You once said he is uncommonly beautiful. So I know this is a very high compliment."

Krista laughed, "I saw Uncle Milo last year. He is still beautiful and he still loves the ladies without melanin. I saw him with two of them in the space of a month while he was here. One of them did not speak English. She kept raking her hands across his chest and murmuring amor amor delicioso."

James chuckled. "The man likes what he likes."

"I figure you two see each other more now that you are in the States?" Krista asked.

"Yes." James nodded. "He is no longer in the army. He lives near me. He started a restaurant and has taken up fishing. I join him when I have the time."

Krista nodded. "Last year, Uncle Milo said you were not

married and didn't even have a girlfriend. He says it keeps him up at nights."

James laughed. "My dad is too interested in my love life. I honestly don't know how he finds the time when his is usually so complicated."

"I wish I had him as a father. He was always so great with you." Krista's eyes clouded over. "Then again, I always just wished I had a father full stop, or at least knew who he was."

"So the search continues, James raised an eyebrow, after all these years, no answers."

Krista nodded. "I even enlisted Sir Reggie to help me. He came up with nothing. I just want a name. I wouldn't even mind if he was as complicated as Uncle Milo."

"I can do without the complicated." James smirked. "My dad's stories can be draining. It keeps me on the straight and narrow with my relationships, though."

Krista smiled. "Two things I remember about you, you always hated complications, and you don't fight for a relationship."

"That's true on one count." James frowned. "When we broke up, you shut me out completely. There was no fighting for our relationship. There is just so much rejection a man can take."

"I wanted you to pursue me, I wanted proof that you felt something." Krista said. "I might have gone a little off the rails with my accusations, but I felt as if a part of you had exited the building. Maybe I was projecting wrongly, but I should have listened to you when you denied that you were involved with that girl."

"I was never involved with Tiana," James said. "You knew it at the time, you chose to believe otherwise."

"I'll be the first to admit I acted rashly," Krista sighed, "and now here we are six years later, you are a big shot television producer, and I went and married a man who I thought loved me with all he had. Only thing is, I was wrong."

"I never knew you got married so soon after…" James' voice trailed away. "I distanced myself from everything that happened here anyway. I put it in a file marked the past and moved on."

"So you never heard from her again, then," Krista asked skeptically.

"You mean, Tiana?" James shook his head. "No."

"I always thought you would have, Krista shrugged, I don't know…"

James looked at his watch and then at the hill. "It's getting light out, and I have to take that hill…"

"I don't want to keep you," Krista said quickly. "Did Aunt Beatrice talk to you?"

"Yes." James nodded. I'll tell my assistant to put you down on the shortlist. You'll have to earn a spot in the final three like the rest of the group though, nothing is guaranteed.

Krista nodded. "Thank you. That is more than I expected after how we ended things."

James shrugged. "I don't hold grudges, Krista. See you later…"

"Wait." Krista bit her lip. "Is there any hope for us? I mean, you are single; I am single…"

James stared at Krista in shock. Surely, she didn't expect them to take up where they left off six years ago?

"We don't know each other anymore, Krista." He chose his words carefully. "I remember when we were friends when we used to run around the great house and through these streets as children. I think I want to hold on to those memories. The relationship bits I would prefer not to revisit. I wouldn't mind friendship, everything else is off the table. We've been there and done that."

Krista looked away from him awkwardly. "Well okay then, if you ever change your mind."

James resisted an emphatic no. He wouldn't change his mind. He didn't want to hurt her feelings further.

"See you around, Krista."

"Yes," Krista cleared her throat, "see you around."

****

It had been a grueling uphill run to the great house. James stopped to catch his breath and sat on the old church steps and looked over at the greenery. For as far as the eye could see there were no buildings, nothing but orange trees. To the east of the property, there were a few greenhouses that blended in with the trees, and directly before him, the view was unspoiled. He figured that the view was the same three hundred years before when the first Morgan built the great house and most of the outer buildings which were still standing.

It had been one of the largest great houses in the area.

The place had been in his uncles' family for several generations from the conquering of the islands by the British. It was still a working plantation, that was vastly diminished from its original acreage. It had spanned nearly three thousand acres in its heyday, mostly producing sugar cane. Now it was oranges.

He took a deep cleansing breath of air and felt the breeze pass over his face. He always felt a tingle of excitement when he came here. He always woke up with a sense of anticipation, the breathless expectancy of what's next dogging his steps.

He jogged back to the great house, eager to start his day. His uncle was financing the miniseries from beginning to end, all he had to do was bring his expertise. This was like a vacation of sorts, and he would treat it as such.

He stretched on the steps, appreciating the sunrise. He had missed this place.

"James." Traci interrupted him in mid-stretch.

She smiled at him happily, "I had the best sleep I've had in ages, there is something about this house."

James grinned. "I know."

"I might even wake up and do the jog thing. I feel that excited."

"I am happy that you love it here, Traci, we'll be here all summer." He pointed to the folder in her hands. "I see you have work for me already."

"Yes," Traci nodded, "I shortlisted the twelve writers based on the samples that were sent."

"Finally." James nodded. "I was thinking of working with four writers instead of three and getting this over quickly, uncle Reggie is anxious."

"Sure thing." Traci nodded.

"Wait, I want to add another name to your list, Beatrice's niece, Krista. She is a writer, has her masters in English. She has lived here for most of her life, and Beatrice begged me to give her a shoo-in."

"Okay, then." Traci nodded, "When you okay the list, I'll shoot the twelve an email. Are we still on for Monday?"

"Yep," James nodded, "no time to waste. May I see the list?"

"Sure." Traci handed him the paper. "I tried for equality, but there are five men and seven women. Now eight since we are adding Krista."

James nodded. "Okay."

"I am going to set up base in the library," Traci said. "I'll join you for breakfast on the patio. I wandered into the kitchen and in there smells divine. I am going to love this gig I tell you." She patted her rounded belly. "And I was thinking of losing some weight this summer. I am definitely going to have to do some jogging because I intend to eat."

James chuckled and looked down at the paper. He perused the names and had to pause at the bottom. Surely, he couldn't be seeing right, Tiana Pryce. How many Tiana Pryce's were in Jamaica?

"Hey, Traci!" He called urgently. Traci had almost reached the heavy entrance door. "About Tiana Pryce, why did you choose her?"

James jogged up the steps and held the door open for Traci.

"Because her story was rife with imagery. She has potential. Why? Do you know her?"

"Maybe." James shrugged. "I once had a student with that name."

"Oh yeah?" Traci grinned. "Intriguing. Because the story was about a handsome teacher, who had a torturous conflicted love for his student. He wanted her so much it almost drove him mad."

"I want to see the sample she sent you." James sighed heavily. "That sounds like Tiana."

Traci nodded. "It was good. I liked it, wouldn't mind reading more. I want to know did the teacher kill himself because of his forbidden thoughts, or did he wait until she grew up to pursue her. I want to ask Tiana what she has planned."

James shook his head. "Just last night I was thinking about her."

"You were?" Traci raised an eyebrow. "Are you the conflicted teacher in this dramatic piece?"

"No." James frowned.

"She described you though." Traci grinned. "The teacher had green eyes, caramel complexion, and he had a cute

English accent. Not that you have much of the accent now…"

"Mr. Dalton, sir." Beatrice interrupted him them before he could utter his denial. "Breakfast will be on the veranda in thirty minutes. Will Mr. Jose be joining you?"

"Thanks, Beatrice, yes he'll be there." He smiled at Beatrice and then turned to glare at Traci.

"Should I take her off the list?" Traci asked sweetly, mock innocence stamped on her face. "I had no idea you two had history."

"No, leave her on," James said grimly, "and send me that sample."

Traci nodded and headed to the library.

He went upstairs and had a quick shower. The day was filled with anticipation. He didn't stop to question why.

****

Beatrice had laid out quite a spread, way too much food for just the three of them. His mother called before he could dig in.

"Honey," she said without preamble. "As you know, I am going back home, and the Wileys are throwing me a send away party. I want you to come, I want them to meet my son. I talk about you a lot."

"I don't know." James dithered. He didn't mind seeing his mother, he saw her infrequently as it was. "I'll come by on Thursday before the party."

"No." His mother said sternly, "and I want to show you off. I already told them you'll be here. If you don't show up, they'll think I have a phantom child. Surely you can spare the time. You haven't started doing anything yet, have you. It's like you are on vacation."

He had thought the same thing moments before, this was a

well-needed vacation, he couldn't deny it now.

"Okay, I'll be there." James couldn't keep the long-suffering resignation from his voice.

He hung up the phone and Traci chuckled. "Can't say no to the mom, huh?"

"Never was able to." James sat down.

Jose laughed heartily. "You are a momma's boy, just like me James."

James shrugged. "Not really, I was more of a grandmother's boy. I grew up with my Nonna, spent most of my childhood with her, down the hill, in the village."

"What happened to your dad?" Traci was the one who asked.

"He flitted between the US and Jamaica. He was a US Marine and sometimes off to some secret mission or the other. Whenever he was here, we spent time together. I saw more of him in my earlier years than I did my mom.

"That changed when I was about twelve years old. She took me to the UK, her husband thought he would be okay with having me around, but he wasn't. I was a constant reminder that his wife had an affair with a black man and had a kid for one. My sisters hated me on sight, and my mother's husband family would openly call me names while I was around. It was a toxic environment to grow up in. I was deeply unhappy, and so was my mother. It was a balancing act for her at the time. It was with great relief that I came back to Jamaica and went to university."

"We should be shooting your life story instead," Jose commented.

James shrugged. "My parents have interesting and complicated relationships. Where do you think I get material from for Secrets of Love? I don't have to look far."

"And because of that complication, you are not into long

term relationships," Traci said, putting on her counsellor voice.

"I was engaged once," James said. "I can do long term. I am just…"

"Holding out for the girl in your head," Traci said softly. "The student who drove you to lust…"

A picture of Tiana floated in his mind's eye. Tiana with the pencil behind her ears and an impish smile on her lips. He would never listen to the song To Sir With Love in a neutral manner again, without thinking about her.

She had always ended her essays with a line from the Lulu song, If you wanted the moon, I would try to make a start, but I would rather you let me give my heart 'To Sir, With Love'

He paused for so long to respond to Traci that she and Jose moved on with the conversation.

"My mom wants me to marry a good Latina woman from a nice family," Jose chuckled "and she'll do the picking. All I need to do is relax. I tell her, Mama, I am going to be the one who lives with your choice. I should choose, relationships take work, I have to know if the female in question is worth it."

"And you are right." Traci nodded. "My parents were the ones who set me up with my ex-husband, and it was a disaster."

"How?" Jose asked. "What happened?"

Traci answered, and James tuned them out.

He tucked into his breakfast, analyzing why he was suddenly preoccupied with Tiana Pryce. Maybe it was the trip down memory lane last night. Maybe it was meeting Krista again this morning. And maybe it was the fact that he was here in Jamaica again and her name was on a list of people he was going to work with in the coming weeks.

Who knew? It wasn't that deep. He shouldn't be dwelling on her. She possibly had changed beyond recognition.

"By the way, James, I sent you that sample from Tiana Pryce." Traci intruded on his thoughts.

"Thanks." He nodded, "I'll check it out later. What's on the itinerary for the day?"

Chapter Seven

You are cordially invited to the Morgan Great House for a writing interview. Unlike the traditional interview format, we will be putting you through some elimination rounds. Please reserve two weeks for the initial rounds. RSVP if you can make it. Accommodation, food, and seminars are free of cost.

Tiana read the text from Traci Black and squealed. “I got in!” She said to Carla who was busy wrapping up her final days at Cannon Publishers.

“I knew you would!” Carla celebrated with her. “Now you have Mr. Oliver to bargain with. If you make it to the final list, you’ll probably need the entire summer.”

“I never thought of that," Tiana said.

“How much are they paying?” Carla asked.

“I have no idea," Tiana whispered.

“It will probably be more than you are making now," Carla grumbled. “It won’t be bad for a summer gig. Just make sure you get to the final two and haggle with Mr. Oliver for six weeks with the hope of an extension."

Tiana nodded. "Haggle. I have never haggled in my life."

"It's easy," Carla said breezily, "Mr. Oliver is a pussycat."

****

A pussycat with claws, Tiana thought when she stumbled out of Mr. Oliver's office after her haggling session earned her a month off with pay and the hope of extending her leave for the summer.

She called Elsa and Giselle and Yara and got a mixed reaction. Giselle was happy for her. Giselle was usually happy for anything that sounded like progress.

Elsa thought she was jeopardizing her job for an unsure thing and Yara was apathetic.

"I knew you'd get shortlisted," Yara muttered. "I just hope James Dalton has aged like milk. I hope he is bald and has bad breath, but knowing you, you'd probably find that attractive once it's James."

Tiana sighed. "You are a real friend, happy for me when I get an opportunity."

Yara snorted, "I hope he is married with six kids one for each year that you haven't seen him."

"I went and read up about him," Tiana said. "He is not married, and he doesn't have children."

"Well then, I hope he lost his penis and is now talking in high soprano."

"Yara!" Tiana gasped. "That's sick!"

"Just promise me you won't break up with Cole until you see James and talk to him and get this madness settled and out of the way."

"I promised you…" Tiana hissed. "I'll keep the promise."

"Okay." Yara sighed. "I guess I should grudgingly wish

you well."

"That would be nice." Tiana chuckled.

****

Tiana had lunch with Cole at his office. It was a week since their big engagement. He had insisted on lunch, but it was obvious that he didn't have the time to sit and talk. When she got there, he was on the phone. She didn't mind sitting and looking around his office. It was aesthetically pleasing. It was where Cole displayed his artwork. Most of them were landscapes a few were of her. Cole loved to paint her.

She had found it flattering at first, but now she fretted what was he going to do with them when they broke up. She was going to do as Yara said, but she was thinking that breaking up with Cole was bordering on the inevitable. But how did you break up with someone who asked for your hand in marriage in such a spectacular fashion. He had the whole church happy for them. Everybody was excited for her and was telling her congratulations. What was she going to say without looking like the villain?

He hung up the phone and smiled at her. "What were you saying about going to St. Ann?"

"I was shortlisted," Tiana explained. "I'd go to the Great House, for the first week, then I'd come back on the weekend. If I am selected for the final six, I'd be there for another week and then if I am a part of the final three, I'll probably spend all of July and some of August there."

"I didn't even know you applied!" Cole raised an eyebrow. "I swear this summer is crazy. I have more business than I can handle, which I will never complain about, but I think this is hurting us. We need some time together. We need to have a serious talk. Maybe go away for a weekend…separate rooms of course. You know what? Why don't we just elope, I can't wait to be with you."

His phone rang again, and he grimaced. "Just my luck."

He answered, then covered the mouthpiece. "Just when I was thinking about how I can finally paint you naked."

Tiana inhaled raggedly.

"I know," Cole murmured. "I don't think I'll have time to paint. We have two years of cold showers to make up for."

Tiana laughed uncomfortably. It sounded fake to her but made no impact on Cole. He went back to his phone call.

She watched him, willing herself to feel something. He was the kind of man a woman would take a second look at and then wonder what kind of lucky woman had his full attention.

He was tall, dark, and handsome. All the Carrs were good looking. Cole looked like a dark Boris Cudjoe.

He was thirty-two years old and had admitted to her that he had been wild in his twenties but was now ready to spend the rest of his life with her.

She had always known him as Yara's big brother and had only started talking to him at Yara's twenty-first birthday party. She had no idea that he had liked her until he told her that night that he could paint her all day, every day and never get bored.

She had loved the attention at first. When Cole was focused on you, it was pretty heady.

Cole's secretary, Bri, knocked on the office door and stuck her head in. "Sorry to interrupt, Cole. Mason Magnus is here. He says it's about a mutual client and some urgent changes."

"Sorry about this, Hun." Cole looked at her, then at Bri, "Ask Mason if he can wait for ten minutes tops. I am on the phone with a client in Canada."

"I'll keep him company," Tiana got up, "and then I'll see

myself out. We'll talk, okay?"

"Okay." Cole blew her a kiss and went back to his call.

"Mason is in the conference room," Bri said, pointing to the door with a long table.

Tiana could see him on his computer through the glass conference doors. Mason Magnus was once one of Yara's crushes. He had been a regular feature in their childhood when his mother was married to Toddy. Yara would act girly and giggle about him. She still had him high up on her list of desirable men. Contrarily, he was high up on Elsa's hit list of undesirables. Elsa had always had an irrational reaction to Mason.

Mason inspired opposite reactions in her friend and her sister. Yara thought he was gorgeous, Elsa thought he was odious.

Tiana had to agree with Yara about Mason. He wasn't blatantly handsome, but he had presence even as a teen. The more you looked at him, the more you got it, the combination of dark skin, pink lips, and piercing eyes.

She pushed the door and went into the room. "Mason M!"

Mason looked up and grinned, "Tiana! How are you? I haven't seen you in a while."

He got up and hugged her and then said ruefully. "You look gorgeous, as usual."

"Thank you." Tiana sat across from him, "You don't look bad yourself. What have you been doing?"

"Changed my glasses." Mason pointed to his glasses. "I am blind without them, but these are still high prescription but less chunky."

"No, that's not it." Tiana smiled. "You look different, more relaxed."

"Maybe." Mason smiled, showing perfectly white teeth. "I am trying to take life a little less seriously these days."

"You?" Tiana raised her eyebrows. "That's a shocker. You are always so intense."

"When you are too high intensity, eventually there is burn out." Mason looked at his watch. "Are you meeting me instead of Cole?"

"No," Tiana shook her head, "Cole is on the phone with a Canadian client. He said he'd be ten minutes."

Mason nodded. "I don't mind once you keep my company. So you and Cole still going strong, huh?"

"Something like that." Tiana change topic quickly. "How is aunty Celine?"

"Great." Mason folded his arms. "She is finally moving on with her life after hurricane Toddy devastated her."

"It has taken her years though," Tiana said softly. "She must have loved Toddy very much."

"When my mother loves, she loves hard." Mason sighed. "If I had a woman who loved me like that, I would not have squandered it like Theodore Pryce did."

"Of all the wives and girlfriends that Toddy had, I miss her the most." Tiana said loyally, "She gave the best advice."

Mason smiled. "Do you still live with him?"

"No," Tiana shook her head, "Giselle moved out first. She bought a house and then had a baby for Pete. They got married last year."

Mason raised an eyebrow. "Peter Wiley?"

"Yep." Tiana nodded.

"Interesting." Mason grinned. "Gis got married first. I always thought you would be the one who got married first and Gis would be the one who got married in her late twenties and then Elsa would be perennially single."

Tiana laughed. "You got it wrong."

"So where do you guys live, since you are no longer under Toddy's thumb?"

"Toddy downgraded to a three-bedroom place, and Giselle's house was empty, so Elsa and I live there now."

Mason smiled cynically. "I know that Toddy has been winding down his extravagant lifestyle. Serves him right."

Tiana cleared her throat. "I know you have a vendetta with Toddy."

"Not really, not anymore." Mason shrugged. "I have him where I want him now."

"He says you are after his senate seat." Tiana linked her fingers together and put on her most earnest expression. "It is the only thing he has left. You took his business, and he had to sell his house and…"

"Is that what the crafty devil told you?" Mason frowned. "He is something else. The business that he sold started out as Pryce and Magnus, that's right. My father was his partner and did the lion's share of the work while Toddy slept his way through contracts. He called it his charm offensive. That mansion that you lived in also belonged to my father. Toddy always coveted the place, when my dad died Toddy got it for less to nothing because a bit of a mortgage was left on it. Even Toddy's senate seat was my father's. Toddy doesn't care about working for the people of this country. He just wanted the prestige of being called a senator.

"And worst of all, Theodore Pryce, seduced my grieving mother, took advantage of her vulnerability and married her and then broke her. He took everything that my father once had. All I am doing is taking them back."

"I see." Tiana swallowed. "Never knew the backstory."

"And why should you?" Mason asked. "Taking care of the three of you was the one good no strings attached thing that Toddy has ever done in his life. That's why I actually went easy on him even though he didn't deserve it. He is ruthless and evil, a bloodsucking narcissist who is always looking out for number one."

"Oh." Tiana opened her mouth and snapped it shut. "To us, Toddy was the only family member who was willing to take us in when we had no one. He is a good man."

"And to me, he was the one who took all that my father worked for, and then if that was not enough, he took my mother and destroyed her."

"I er…" Tiana shook her head; she had never thought of Toddy as being a ruthless destroyer, it was unsettling.

"So how is Elsa these days?" Mason changed the topic, knowing that he had shocked Tiana. "Is she still the hellcat that she used to be, or has she grown up?"

"She's still take-me or leave-me Elsa," Tiana said faintly. "She is at an advertising conference at the Palm Hotel in Montego Bay."

"Oh," Mason folded his arms, "I am heading there now, giving a guest speech. Maybe I'll see her."

"Maybe." Tiana looked at the clock. "I have to get some lunch, one way or the other. I hope Cole comes by soon. It was nice seeing you again, Mason."

Mason nodded. "Likewise. Take care Tiana."

"You too." Tiana left the building and then headed in the direction of the Wiley Complex. She had a hankering for some Yum Yum food and Yara's company. She needed to distract herself from hearing those awful things about Toddy.

Chapter Eight

Tiana drove into the Wiley Complex a little after seven on Thursday night and parked in front of Guy's townhouse. She had to pick up Ethan as promised, and though she wasn't looking forward to interacting with Liz Morgan, she was anticipating spending time with her sweet, innocent, uncomplicated nephew.

Mason's revelations about Toddy had disturbed her. She didn't want to think of Toddy as a ruthless businessman who had ruined the Magnus family, but not even Yara's chatter or a couple pages of work could distract her.

She had learned something today. Something she knew before but never took the time to ruminate over. People had different sides; a cold-blooded killer probably had a partner he would die to protect. A gentle family man could be a rapist. An arrogant pig of a boss could be a tender lover at home. Everything depended on the place you held in that person's life. She knew Toddy as a warm, loving family man and she was going to go with that. Yes, she knew he had a wandering eye, and he loved women, but she didn't see much of that growing up. Most of it she read in the gossip section of the papers.

She inhaled and then exhaled pushing it all out of her mind. Then she got out of her car, walked up the brick-lined walkway, and knocked on the door. It was dragged opened after a pause, and Lizzette Morgan stood there. She was on the phone.

"Okay honey, I am looking forward to it," Liz said to the person on the phone.

She hung up the phone and smiled widely, "Tiana! Pete said you are taking Ethan for the evening."

"Yes." Tiana nodded.

"Come on in." Liz opened the door wider. "I feel as if for all the time I have been here that I rarely speak to you."

Tiana cleared her throat, "well... er…"

"I know you are busy." Liz grinned at her. "You young people are always busy. I may not speak to you, but I see you regularly, though."

"What?" Tiana asked, confused.

"I visit the gallery regularly, and I bought a painting of you. I had it right there." Liz pointed at an empty spot on the wall, "you were standing beside a strawberry trellis. It is a lovely rendition of you, the artist, Cole Carr is seriously talented, and he had a beautiful subject, of course."

"That was my sister's wedding at Guy's farm," Tiana said weakly. "I had no idea Cole sold it."

"Oh, yes, he did. I convinced him." Liz smiled. "Would you like some tea?"

"Yes, thank you," Tiana said cautiously.

"Have a seat, have a seat," Liz said, indicating to one of the settees in the open plan living room.

"Where is Ethan?" Tiana looked around; the place was quiet.

"I sent him over to Shawn's house." Liz smiled. "You can pick him up there, Ethan and Cairo will be tight when they grow up. He was crying when Shawn came to pick up Cairo, so I told her to take him too."

Tiana gritted her teeth. So that meant she could have avoided Liz. She looked over at Liz, as she busied herself with the tea. She was an attractive woman who was in her fifties. She had light brown hair which she kept long, and a slim toned body which came from hours of walking about. Liz loved to walk. She even walked in the more unsavory areas in Kingston quite oblivious to the dangers, or at least that was what Giselle told her.

Liz carried the tray over to Tiana and sat across from her. "I am so excited."

"Why?" Tiana asked.

"My son is here in Jamaica. He is a television producer, you know."

Tiana took up her teacup and sipped the liquid. She was doing it to keep her hand occupied. She was not a tea drinker. She didn't like hot beverages never had.

Liz obviously loved it though, she sipped the tea and then closed her eyes in delight.

"It's amazing how things worked out for him. He was involved in some bad business that happened while he was a teacher. It was not his fault, and they dismissed him wrongfully, but he bounced back. Some things happen in life for a reason, and you have to endure them for a season."

Tiana fidgeted with the teacup. Why on earth was she here? She tensed, waiting for Liz to bring up what the bad business was, but Liz brushed over that.

"James is my only boy; I want to see him happy and settled

in a good marriage with a woman that loves him, and he loves her just as much. My family is not known for good marriages. I hope he breaks the trend. A mother can hope."

Tiana cleared her throat. "Well, I think I should…

"No, don't leave, Liz widened her eyes. "Here I am babbling about my son. He'd be mortified if he heard me."

"Tell me more about you, Tiana. I can't believe I'll be leaving soon, and we never really talked. And we should have been friends. After all, you are in the publishing business and Giselle said you were a writer."

Tiana blinked rapidly. "I am not a writer; I haven't published anything."

"But you write, that makes you a writer." Liz smiled, "I don't think there is a definition that says that writers have to be published. My son is a writer, but he writes scripts for television. He will not take my suggestions to alter his shows."

Tiana chuckled. "Why won't he?"

"Because he says I am too over the top," Liz grunted. "I am chuffed about him doing so well. It could have gone differently for him, but God works in mysterious ways, doesn't he?"

Tiana nodded. She ignored the voice that told her to not ask any unnecessary questions about James Dalton and found herself asking. "How did he get into the television business?"

"He was a teacher, an excellent one." Liz said fondly, "and then he had an over-enthusiastic student who derailed his career."

Liz paused and sipped her tea. "Frankly I can't blame the student, James is spectacular to look at. He's a lighter shade of his father who is glorious. He inherited my green eyes, but that's all he inherited from me; he could be Milo Dalton's twin."

Liz grinned playfully." Milo will make a woman forget herself, her marriage and her principles. I met him while here on holiday. I was visiting my brother Reginald, and I saw Milo on a motorcycle in the neighborhood.

"One look and I was paralyzed. He is pure masculinity. I had never been so attracted to a man as I was to him. It didn't take long for me to find out his name and where he lived, and I stalked him."

Tiana gasped. It sounded similar to how she had pursued James.

"Yes, I was pathetic." Liz giggled girlishly. "I completely forgot about my family in the UK. My husband called and I told him I was not coming home. Of course, I had to go back since Milo didn't live here. He was a marine and had to return to the States. I had to tell my husband I was pregnant with Milo's baby."

"Really?" Tiana squeaked.

"Really." Liz shook her head. "My husband was livid at first. I had to promise to give the baby to Milo's mother when he was born. I messed up my son's life with my choices. Liz sighed. Anyway, we were talking about his big break in the television industry."

Tiana was nodding like a marionette. She wouldn't have minded hearing more about James Dalton's history. She wondered if he felt like an outcast and what his relationship with his mother was like.

"So after the student got him fired," Liz continued, "he had to leave school accommodation the same day. He had no job and nowhere to live, and Krista dumped him. Krista was his fiancé at the time. I thought he had gotten engaged too early. I wasn't especially sad to see that relationship end.

"Anyway, James called me confused. I still remember the

hurt in his voice. A mother never wants to hear that."

Tiana swallowed. She felt prickles of guilt jabbing her. She couldn't look Liz in the eyes.

"And then I called my brother, Reggie, who has contacts everywhere and he got him a job with a production house in the States. James started his own thing a year later. Did some great series and the rest they say is history. He found his calling. He is right where he should be now."

"That's amazing." Tiana cleared her throat. "So er… does that mean he has forgiven the girl that got him fired? It seems as if he did quite well for himself after that."

"Girls are always throwing themselves at James." Liz chuckled. "It may have been a blessing; his life did take another trajectory, and he loves what he does now. It makes him happy, which makes me happy."

Tiana worried her lower lip. Should she confess that she was the student that got him fired? It sounded as if Liz could relate, she had stalked Milo Dalton.

The moment was lost when Liz's phone rang. She got up to take the call, which sounded like her flight arrangements.

Tiana got up and waved goodbye when it seemed as if Liz was going to take a while.

Liz covered the phone and winked at her. "If you come by early on Sunday, you could get a one on one with James. It would be a fabulous opportunity for you."

Tiana gasped. Sunday! She was going to see James Dalton on Sunday!

No, she was not going to come by early to meet him, she already had nightmares about meeting him for this job interview. She wasn't going to open herself up to it ending when he realized that it was her.

She waved to Liz and let herself out.

She had to drop off Ethan for the picture taking, and then

she would remain as inconspicuous as possible.

****

James was in the middle of an interesting conversation with Jordan Wiley about the premise of the miniseries when Tiana entered the pool area. She was dressed in an off the shoulder white dress, which showed off an expanse of smooth shoulder skin. Her hair was in a casual top knot off her face. She looked fresh and pretty. Her eyelashes were still sooty and long.

He inhaled audibly.

Jordan followed his gaze and grinned. "I have heard that reaction before. People can't help it."

"She's beautiful," James said simply. He looked at the little boy that was with her. He looked very much like Jordan Wiley. He looked from her to the kid and then back at Jordan.

He was confused, Jordan had introduced him to a very pretty lady named Shawn earlier and said she was his wife.

They had looked very much in love. They had a little boy around the same age as the one Tiana was holding on to. What was Tiana doing here, and who was the child?

"That child looks so much like you," James murmured.

"I know," Jordan said wryly, "he also looks like his father, who is my nephew."

"His father?" James raised eyebrows. "So er the pretty girl is your cousin, and she has a child with your nephew? It sounds disturbing."

Jordan laughed. "They are not related. Different branches of the family. We have an interesting family history, like yours."

"Oh," James said in relief. He still felt strangely disappointed that Tiana had a child.

“Is she married to your nephew?” James asked, regretting it as he asked. He had asked with too much interest.

Jordan looked at him knowingly. “No, she is not married to my nephew. Her sister Giselle is.”

“Good," James said solemnly. “She is not engaged, is she or otherwise entangled in any relationships?”

“She got engaged recently,” Jordan shrugged. “Her fiancé had the choir sing the Byrds song, Turn, Turn, Turn.”

“I know that song.” James felt a sense of deflation. “It’s actually one of my favorite Bible chapters.”

It certainly had kept him through the good times and the bad times. None of those states lasted forever.

“A time for everything,” Jordan murmured. “I like it too. I wouldn’t have thought of proposing to someone with it.”

“It was quite creative.” James nodded.

“Cole Carr is in hot demand around town,” Jordan said. “He is an artist, a graphic designer and is quite the creative person. We send him quite a bit of business from our firm. He is good.”

Tiana likes creative men. James thought but didn’t say out loud.

“You should go over and say hello. Introduce yourself,” Jordan said in the silence.

“I will.” James nodded. He didn’t mention that he would meet Tiana tomorrow in any case or that he already knew her.

Anticipation zinged in his blood as he looked at her again. This was it, today they were meeting as equals.

No student-teacher relationship to muddy the waters.

****

Tiana did not consider herself to be a good actress. She

wasn't particularly good at hiding her feelings or projecting feelings that she wasn't feeling.

And today, she was nervous.

James Dalton was standing forty steps from where she was. He was in a white shirt that showed off his biceps every time he raised his hand to take a sip of whatever was in his cup. He looked cool and casual, and just as she remembered.

She was staring, she couldn't drag her eyes away. This was how it had started all those years ago.

He had walked into the classroom, and her heart had taken flight beating at an irregular rate, and everything else had faded around her. She had become hyper-aware of herself, of her feelings. It was as if everything else ceased to exist when James Dalton was in the same room with her.

The feeling was back.

She inhaled raggedly.

Yup, here was the spark. The feeling that had eluded her for six years, the feeling that she wished she had even a tiny iota of for Cole. It was back in full force.

Then his eyes met hers. How could they not?

In the past, when she had stared at him long enough, he had always turned around to look at her too. Back then, she was met with stony rejection. This time, he didn't drag his eyes away. This time, he held her gaze.

He raised his cup in greeting.

He recognized her. Tiana panicked. Was he going to announce to the entire gathering that she was the girl who had stalked him out of a job, and had written him long embarrassing messages in high school?

She was the one who dragged her eyes away from the impossibly long staring exercise they were undergoing.

She looked longingly across the hibiscus hedges to the parking lot. Ethan was in good hands; he was among family.

There was no reason why she had to stay at the party, she could always leave or hide out in her car. She would come back in two or three hours, but how was she going to work with James Dalton or prove that she was now mature and sophisticated if she ran and hid.

She would be seeing him tomorrow anyway.

She inhaled raggedly, nervousness tying a knot in her belly. She should have taken a couple of Elsa's hemp gummies to calm herself before attending the party. Then she would be zen and not skittish or act like a seventeen-year-old girl who had just discovered that just one look from a man could make her feel as if fire was walking along her skin.

She was bigger than this. She was older now. More mature, hopefully. Her feet were not obeying her as she scurried toward the parking lot, cursing the length of her dress and her cute itty-bitty sandals with just a slim strap on her big toe. They weren't made for escaping from past crushes.

"Tiana." She stopped suddenly as if his voice was a shot. He hadn't even spoken loudly, but it was enough to stop all action around her.

He still had the faintest British accent. He pronounced her name Tea Anna. It still managed to cause a little shiver along her spine. She used to go to bed, imagining him whispering her name in the dark. No one would ever know the depths of her obsession. And neither would he, she turned around slowly and plastered a smile on her face.

"Hi, er…"

James chuckled. He didn't even bother to supply his name. He knew she was acting.

"Where are you running off to?"

"I just dropped off my nephew," Tiana said her voice sounding trembly. "I er, I can come back later for him."

Deep breaths, Tiana. Deep breaths. She kept repeating in

her head.

He walked even closer to her. She looked behind; her car was ten paces close. The privacy fence to the poolside meant that nobody could see them from where they were.

“I had no idea you knew my mother,” his voice was husky, “or that she was working for your family. Life is strange, isn't it?”

“It is.” Tiana nodded briskly. Or what she thought was briskly. She was acting like a nervous wreck. “I should go.”

“No.” He frowned at her. “We need to talk, clear the air, don’t you think?”

“Well I, I guess we do.” Tiana clasped her hands together because they were trembling. “I am sorry about the er back in high school, I was a…”

She stared into his limpid green eyes and then realized that they were more blue-green than just green. She had lost her train of thought.

“High school?” James prompted softly.

“Yes, high school. Please forgive me.” Tiana licked her lips. He followed her tongue with his gaze. The air between them was charged. “I did stupid stuff. I was stupid. Can I just say I am sorry, I have felt guilty about it for years. You lost your job and your fiancé and everything because of me.”

“Apology accepted.” James smiled. “There is nothing to forgive, really. I was mad at you for a very small, infinitesimal point in time, but I was madder at myself. I shouldn’t have met you in my office alone. If I hadn't, there would have been no kiss and no pictures and none of the subsequent events.”

“You sure there is no lingering resentment?” Tiana asked tentatively.

“Nope. None.” James held out his hand for a handshake, and she reluctantly put hers in his.

It was a big mistake. Touching him was like touching a

live wire, a shock to her system.

"Friends?" He asked huskily, "we'll be working together for a while, do you think we can forget about the past?"

"Yes." Tiana said, her voice sounding squeaky, "I sure can. I am a professional, and mature, and settled. I even have a fiancé."

She was using Cole as a crutch to make her seem more mature. This was it, she had really gone and done it.

James took his time to release her hand, and all her fingers were tingling.

Tiana struggled to look him in the face. "So, I will see you tomorrow?"

"Looking forward to it." James' eyes lingered at her ring less fingers.

"I left my ring at home," Tiana said, "I can't remember to wear it. The engagement is fairly new, he had a choir sing the proposal. Then he got down on one knee…"

She was rambling one thing after another while James' eyebrows went higher and higher after every citation.

"I heard." James nodded. "Are you happy?"

No! Tiana wanted to say.

She nodded mutely instead.

"Well then, I wish you the absolute best."

"Thank you, James." She whispered.

James smiled at her slowly. His eyes intently boring into hers, observing how nervous he was making her.

"You remember my name, after all."

"I probably will never forget it." Tiana laughed uncomfortably. "You had quite an impact on me."

"How long have you and your fiancé been together?" James asked, roughly.

"Two years." Tiana inhaled and then exhaled. Her breath caught in her throat as he stepped even closer to her. She could smell his aftershave.

"You don't seem excited about him," James murmured. "Something is missing."

"You don't know that!" Tiana gasped. "How could you…"

"I know when you are excited about somebody," James said. "You are not sure about this guy."

"I was young and slightly stupid in high school." Tiana looked behind her at the sweet escape that was her car. "I short-circuited then. Now I am in a calm, peaceful…"

"Passionless relationship and you frown at being reminded about the time when you were fire and eagerness, with unfettered enthusiasm for a man," James finished her statement. "I understand."

"What's your fiancé's name again?" James asked.

"Why?" Tiana was stinging from his accurate summation of her current condition and her status with Cole.

"Just because…" James looked at her ring finger again. "I want to know."

"Cole Carr," Tiana supplied her voice trembling. "His name is Cole Carr."

"Do you write him long love letters, follow him a discrete distance when he goes home and tell him that you love him every single day, without fail?" James asked, teasing her.

"No!" Tiana shouted.

"No?" James grinned. "Your poor fiancé is missing out."

"He is missing nothing." Tiana inhaled to steady herself. "I am a grown woman; I no longer resort to childish things."

"I don't know," James said. "As an adult, that kind of thing can be heady to a person that you are getting married to. I mean, if he feels the same about you, it would be something else."

"Listen, Mister Dalton…James, you said we should keep the past in the past. I am looking forward to the opportunity to work with you, our personal lives are off-limits."

"Is that so?" James gave her a sexy, half-smile.

She gasped in disbelief. Was he flirting with her? James Dalton was flirting with her. This was a dream come true. Maybe she was dreaming.

It had never happened before. She couldn't even remember if she had ever seen him smile. In high school she was treated to many variations of his glowers.

"Well, I will see you tomorrow." She walked away in what she thought was a dignified manner. Unfortunately, her fancy one strap sandal fell apart. She hopped on one foot to her car. Only daring to look back when she was almost at the driver's door. James was standing where she left him. He hadn't moved.

He was laughing at her.

Tiana sat in the car like a petulant child for the rest of the party.

Chapter Nine

Her phone was ringing somewhere in the distance, Tiana could hear it as if it were far away. She opened one eye, glanced at the clock, and then jumped up. It was seven! It was late! Where was her phone?

She spotted it on the nightstand and answered groggily. "Hello."

"Just checking in," Giselle said brightly, "I heard Ethan spent the night with you."

"Yes!" Tiana gasped. She jumped out of bed and sprinted to the guest room. Ethan was not in the crib. Did he climb out?

"I… er… Gis," she said breathlessly, "I have to go I am late."

"For what?" Giselle asked.

"The job interview with JD Productions."

"Ah." Giselle chuckled. "You can't be that late. I want to talk to my baby, put the phone on speaker."

"Wait a second." Tiana ran through the upstairs rooms like a madwoman and then downstairs. How would he reach downstairs?

Her heart somersaulted in fear. What if someone took their precious baby. Giselle and Pete would roast her. Scoop out her ashes and stomp it on the ground.

"Tiana," Gis sing-songed, "What's happening?"

Tiana rushed to the kitchen and slumped on the island. Elsa had him in her arms, cooing, and singing.

"One sec." Tiana put the phone on speaker.

"How's my baby?" Giselle asked her son.

He squealed in response, touching the phone and trying to get out of Elsa's hand.

"What's wrong with you?" Elsa asked after they spoke to Giselle and she hung up. "You look frazzled."

"I thought somebody had kidnapped Ethan or something. I was sound asleep, the phone rang, I couldn't find him." Tiana ran her fingers through her hair several times. "What a way to shock me awake."

"Nope, no kidnapping. Just me." Elsa sighed. "I got fired yesterday evening, so I am back before the scheduled time. Guess who I saw at the seminar?"

Tiana grunted. She had still not recovered.

"Mason Magnus." Elsa made a face. "Is it me, or is he looking better? Dare I say almost handsome. Not just handsome, but in a sexy librarian kind of way. Who would have thought that I would say that about the weird twerp?"

Tiana laughed.

"I wanted to say but I think he was avoiding me." Elsa mused. "Was his voice always so smooth and soothing? I was not tempted to sleep once in his talk."

"Yes!" Tiana nodded. "You should hear Yara go on and on about him."

"Hmm." Elsa opened the refrigerator and stood there for a while with Ethan inspecting the contents and discussing the merits of what they should eat.

"Why did you lose your job?" Tiana sat down at the island and cupped her head and tried to keep her eyes opened, she was still feeling a little loopy. Maybe if she hadn't tossed and turned through half the night with one romantic dream after another starring James Dalton, she would feel rested now.

"Oh that." Elsa looked at her. "I refused the advances of my boss, and that is putting what I did mildly."

"Your boss is a woman," Tiana murmured. "I thought she was straight."

"Wendy is straight. I am talking about her boss, everyone's boss, the owner of the company Geo King."

"Oh." Tiana widened her eyes. "What happened?"

"He came to the seminar. It was the schmoozing day when all the bigwigs in the industry appear. By the way, Mason gave a great speech. It would make a nice TED talk."

"Ooh, Mason Magnus." Tiana chuckled. "He seems to have suddenly gone up several notches in your estimation."

"Yes well, I guess I was blind in the past. It's as if I am just seeing him now." Elsa shrugged. "Anyway, I was sitting in a quiet area, tired of the schmoozing and Geo threw his hands around me and decided to start nibbling on my ear."

"And?" Tiana widened her eyes.

"I panicked." Elsa shrugged, "punched him in the nose. I think I broke it. I heard a sickening crunch."

"Serve him right." Tiana grinned. "Your self-defense classes are paying off?"

"Yup." Elsa placed Ethan in his highchair and kissed him on the forehead. "Hey Snookums, your aunty is out of a job. She broke her boss' nose."

"Mama," Ethan said, pinching Elsa's cheek.

"I am not your mama," Elsa grinned at him, "but I do wish I had her bank account. I could break noses without fretting about being destitute."

Tiana laughed. "Pete will be by to pick him up this morning and don't worry about the job, you'll get one easy, you rose in the ranks of the advertising business as if you had wings."

"How much of that was because I was good, or how much of it was because of my looks?" Elsa asked troubled. "While licking my neck last night, Geo implied that I got hired because I was hot."

"But you are good at what you do, you love this!" Tiana defended her sister. "I hope you don't internalize this madness."

"No," Elsa shook her head, "I won't."

"Don't let him get him in your head," Tiana said briskly. "Call up Toddy, he has contacts. You can get another job in no time or better yet ask Mason for a job."

"That will be last resort." Elsa snorted, "I am done with favors. I am going to get my next job on my own merits. No Toddy. No Mason. No Cole. You know your boyfriend is well-connected everyone in the industry does business with him."

"Uh," Tiana groaned.

Elsa grinned. "How did last night go? Did you see James Dalton?"

"Yes," Tiana nodded, "and I acted like a fool."

"What else is new?" Elsa murmured. "Is he still scrumptious?"

"Yes." Tiana snorted, "how can I act like I am not hopelessly attracted to the man? I need help if I am going to be working with him."

"Mmm," Elsa rubbed her chin, "I would love to see you try. You never could do it in high school."

"And now I am an adult! I should act blasé and calm and unaffected and not let him get under my skin. And why does he have to be so…him?"

"Uh oh." Elsa grinned.

"This is serious." Tiana sighed. "I said yes to Cole's engagement proposal while I am doubtful with a capital D. Then James Dalton comes into my life, and I still feel like a stupid teenager panting at his every word.

"I promised Yara I would burnout from my system whatever I had for James when I meet him again, and then I'll have a better perspective. How can I do that when after one meeting, I feel as if six years were just yesterday? I am once again a hopeless schoolgirl crushing on her hot teacher."

"How can you still feel the same? You are grown. You are different." Elsa frowned. "It's the same with Gis. She was fixated on Pete for years and then you and James Dalton. What's the matter with the two of you?"

"I don't know." Tiana slowly butted her head on the wall. "At least Gis had reason to be focused on Pete, he was in her life, he liked her back. They saw each other all the time. There is no rhyme or reason for my behavior."

"You can get through the next couple of days," Elsa said philosophically. "Tell yourself James is just a man like any other. You have a man in your life that loves you and would take a bullet for you, think about him instead."

Tiana closed her eyes tightly. "I don't feel the same about Cole. I never did. There is this pressure from everybody to marry him, but…" she opened her eyes, "Els, there is nothing there. I pray about it. The more I pray the more I feel as if he is not the one. I can't see what everybody else is seeing.

"I can't feel it. When I said yes to his shock engagement, I did it because I didn't want to embarrass him in front of all our friends, he had them practicing the song behind my back.

It would look odd for me to say no."

"Point taken." Elsa looked at her keenly, "I don't want to be added to your pressure list. Maybe your lack of feeling is your answer to prayers. Don't force this."

"I won't. I'll try not to." Tiana exhaled. "Thank you for understanding, I sometimes feel confused about this. I ask myself time and time again, what is wrong with me. I am next to lukewarm with Cole, but James Dalton lights a fire inside me that is frightening."

Elsa hugged her around the neck and then kissed her in her hair. "Girl, I can't imagine having that kind of emotional turmoil about any man, but know this, you are my sister, my womb buddy and my friend and you are going to be professional and treat this interview like a serious adult and not a lovesick schoolgirl, you hear me."

"Yes, ma'am." Tiana chuckled.

"Let James Dalton do the chasing if there is any chasing to be done. You will not show one iota of weakness even if he makes you weak-kneed."

****

Tiana repeated Elsa's advice in her head while she drove to St Ann. She was going to treat this interview process like serious business. Except she didn't start off the day professionally.

She was late. Her GPS stopped working when she hit the town, and she had to take directions from some happy locals who gleefully told her the great house was up the hill just around the corner.

By the time she had driven for thirty minutes and was convinced she was lost, she happened upon civilization. She saw little neat houses and what looked like a small-town square. She asked a shopkeeper where the Morgan great house was and finally got an answer.

"Five miles from here," The shopkeeper, a pleasant lady, said. "That's just about seven minutes up the hill."

"Thank you," Tiana said with heartfelt gratitude. She was going to be one hour late. Quite an impression she was making with her new mature attitude.

She drove up the hill, the higher she got, the more pleasant the air felt, and the lovelier the views. She almost stopped to take it all in, but the closer she got, the more nervous she felt.

She didn't have time to sightsee.

She followed the road that led up to a winding driveway and a well-preserved great house in white brick. She followed the sign that said, 'to parking lot' and parked beside an old-style grey Aston Martin. It looked like something out of a James Bond movie.

"Wow," she said out loud.

"I know, right. It is a wow kind of car," A voice said behind her. "It's nice to see a woman admiring old cars."

She spun around. A tall, lean man with tousled black hair and green eyes was eying her up and down.

"Now I think it is my time to say wow," he smiled at her. "The name is Brian Morgan. What's yours?"

"Tiana Pryce," Tiana smiled at him, "and I am late. Do you know where the rest of the writers are meeting?"

"I think they are getting settled in," Brian said. "There should be someone at the main house who can tell you what to do."

He looked at her three-inch heel shoes which she had thought had been a good idea at the time. "I hope you carried more comfortable shoes than that?"

"Yes," Tiana said sheepishly. "I did."

"Let me walk you up to the house," Brian said gallantly. "I

wouldn't want you to twist your ankle."

"Thank you." Tiana beamed at him. "I wouldn't want to show up for my first day of an interview in slippers, sneakers or flats. I thought heels would look more businesslike."

"But this isn't a conventional interview. I think if JD Productions requires you to come all the way into deep rural Jamaica that they should expect you to show up in wellies and jeans."

Tiana started walking, there was a paved walkway which led up to the house.

"It is very lovely here. The view is amazing. Unspoiled. I can see all the way down to the sea."

"I know." Brian smiled at her, "I never get tired of it. That's why I try to come here every weekend. My father appreciates the visits, and I get to take in nature at its finest."

"Who is your father?" Tiana asked.

Brian looked at her in amazement before he answered. "Sir Reginald Morgan, the owner of the place. He inherited it from his father, I am the oldest child, one day I'll inherit it from him."

"Oh," she nodded, "that's nice."

Brian laughed. "You seem unimpressed. I like that."

"I didn't read up enough on the Morgan family," Tiana said fretfully. "I wonder if that will matter. I was so caught up in the eighteenth-century history, I forgot to look up the ownership stuff. I am sure when I hear how rich and influential you are, I'll be suitably impressed."

Brian laughed. "You'll be fine. I think it's the eighteenth-century story that will be important anyway. My father finds it fascinating."

Tiana looked at him warmly. "You are nice."

"That's what my mother says." Brian grinned. "She says her greatest accomplishment is that she grew 'nice' boys.

What do you do in Kingston?"

"I am an editor at Cannon Publishers." Tiana smiled. "What do you do?"

"Property dealer." Brian grinned, "It's nothing as exciting as what James does, though."

"Are you and James close?" Tiana murmured. They were directly in front of the great house now.

"Yes, we always find time for each other over the years. At the moment I am a tad bit jealous that he is going to get to work with you. Maybe I should spend a week up here and offer my help. I could carry your water or something."

Tiana smiled. "And who would run your property empire?"

"There is that," Brian chuckled, "maybe I could exchange places with James, but I can't write to save a life, and I know nothing about the television industry. I guess I shall just stick with what I know."

Tiana laughed. "That would be advisable. You…"

The front door was wrenched open in mid-sentence, and James stood at the entrance.

He looked at the two of them with a scowl on his face. "Tiana, you are late. We'll be having a meet and greet soon. Everybody else has gotten the house tour."

"I am sorry." Tiana swallowed nervously. He looked so good. He was in a green polo shirt that match his eyes. "I had trouble with my GPS, so I had trouble finding this place."

"Hopefully, I'll see you soon, Tiana," Brian said under his breath. "Break a leg. Is that a thing you say to writers?"

"I don't know," Tiana whispered back. "Bye, Brian. It was lovely to meet you."

She walked up the steps to where James was standing. "I am so sor…"

"Save it." James snapped. "Follow me."

She looked back at Brian, who had a grin on his face. He

waved to her as she followed James.

James stopped in the foyer and turned to her. “Stay away from Brian.”

“But he is so funny and friendly and interesting.” Tiana grinned. “You sound so jealous.”

“I am not jealous, Brian is charming yes, but he is also gay. I wouldn’t want you to fall for his flattery and then become disappointed when you find out he doesn’t bat for your team.” James scowled at her. “Besides, I thought you had a fiancé?”

“Yes, I… I do…” Tiana stuttered.

“My mother showed me one of his paintings.” James made a face. “He is good. Are you his only subject?”

“No.” Tiana frowned. “I er…”

James scowled. “I convinced my mother to give me the one she had of you.”

“You did?” Tiana whispered. “Why?”

“I liked it.” James looked at her, intently. “Let’s go.”

Chapter Ten

They entered a large conservatory at the back of the house that was filled with orchids. A sitting area was to the far left that had comfortable looking sofas arranged in a circle. Quite a few persons were sitting and talking.

"This is Sir Reggie's favorite room. He comes here to relax. There are two hundred and twenty species of orchids in here," James said, "his grandfather was a botanist, but he fell in love with orchids and studied them all of his life."

"It's gorgeous," Tiana whispered. "They seem to be all blooming at the same time."

"Not really, it's just that there are so many of them." There is one particular orchid that stands out." James pointed at a plant that had several spikes blooming at the same time. This one is the princess orchid; pretty, flamboyant and she smells sweet too."

Tiana looked at the orchid then at him. "The princess orchid?"

"Yes, Princess." James winked. "Let's introduce you to the others and let the fun begin."

Tiana nodded absently staring at the princess orchid, James was right the orchid was outstanding with the numerous blooming spikes, but had he just called her princess too?

"Everyone this is Tiana Pryce," James said, dragging her attention back to the gathering. "She had trouble finding us like so many of you did, but she is late. We will forgive her this one time."

It was a varied group of people, different ages, but they were mostly women. The men looked at her with avid interest. One girl glared at her with such venom Tiana almost took a step back from the viciousness of the stare.

She wanted to look away, but her eyes kept coming back to the amber-eyed stare.

They had almost identical eye colors, and she seemed familiar. Maybe it was because she looked like a younger version of her older sister Caroline. This girl had the same dark skin and light Pryce eyes, the same nose and mouth. The more she looked at her, the more familiar she felt.

The girl was the first to look away, but Tiana kept staring. She was introduced to everybody by their first names, Linda, Margot, Keisha, Lincoln, Calvin, Hillary, Bradford, Faith, Carl, Josette, Lesley, Craig and then Krista.

Hostile Krista would have been a better title.

Tiana shrugged it aside and said in her friendliest voice. "You look so much like the Pryce side of my family. You look so much like my sister Caroline it is uncanny."

"Oh, really?" Krista said without interest.

Tiana recoiled at the unfriendliness she saw flashing from her eyes.

"Krista's surname is indeed Pryce," James said. "You two can explore that later. For now, Tiana you need to meet Traci and Jose, they'll be judging your work."

Tiana dragged her eyes from Krista and then to Traci, a pleasant face woman who was a bit overweight. She didn't look like the dragon that Tiana was expecting. She wore long, purple braids that matched her purple shirt.

Her smile invited Tiana to smile back. She was refreshingly friendly after her war of the eyes with Krista.

"I want to read the end of that teacher story you sent in." Traci grinned. "Please don't give up on it. It was intriguing."

"Thank you." Tiana smiled. "I won't."

Krista made a rude sound. Tiana was afraid to look around at her.

James did though and gave her a warning look.

"And Jose Garcia," James said. "He is an experienced scriptwriter and will be heading up the writing team."

Tiana shook hands with Jose. He didn't look like a history professor or a writer. He looked like a telenovela heartthrob, with his deep brown eyes and overlong hair that looked artfully tousled.

Tiana sat in a comfy chair far enough away from Krista that she could relax. The lady beside her smiled politely and whispered. "I was one of those who was lost too. Good thing I left out much earlier."

Tiana smiled back, no hostility there, thank God. She had gotten more than she had bargained from Krista who looked like family but hated her for whatever reason.

"Now that we have all been introduced," James said. "I don't want to take up your precious time. There are thirteen of you now, three persons will be chosen from this pool of writers to write the twelve-episode miniseries I have tentatively entitled Love in the Sun."

"If you can come up with a better name, feel free to make your suggestions. The initial naming of shows don't usually stick."

"This will be the format of this interview. You have five days to individually write a one-hour pilot for this historical miniseries. A one-hour pilot is roughly sixty pages. Consider each page to be a minute."

"My uncle, Sir Reginald, will come by shortly to give you a rundown of what the miniseries will be based on. He will be a fourth judge on this venture. This project is near and dear to his heart, so I beg of you, make it hard for us to choose the pilot."

Traci stepped forward. "After the pilot is chosen, seven of you will be culled, leaving six. You will then be split into two groups of three. The group that writes the best first episode based on the pilot will be our writing team."

"James and I will be joining the remaining three," Jose said, "and hopefully we can get it done by the end of August. By the way, the process is usually not as simple as we make it sound, but it's doable. And Sir Reggie will be paying us handsomely for our efforts."

A tall, heavily tanned man who looked a little like the singer Sting walked into the room while Jose was talking. He cleared his throat, and Jose chuckled.

"And he is right here, just in time to confirm it."

The writers laughed. Tiana joined in. Sir Reggie seemed to be an affable gentleman. He had dirty blond hair that was cut in a short-side-long-top style. With a name like Sir Reginald, to her he looked younger than she thought he would. He looked to be in his early fifties. He had a twinkle in his green eyes and a happiness about him that was contagious.

"Ladies and gents, I am so pleased you are here. I have always wanted to do a television soap based on my family. I personally think that they are more interesting and truer than the popular great house fairy tales like the white witch of Rose Hall.

“Did you know the legend of Annie Palmer was based on a fictional book? There is no truth to it whatsoever, the original story is somewhat less interesting than a woman who killed her husbands, had sex with her male slaves, and tortured the female ones.”

“It wasn’t true?” The lady beside her gasped.

"Oh, yes,” Sir Reggie said. “However, my family’s story, set in the 1800s is true. The information has been independently authenticated, and it lines up with family records. I have made the information available at the library, you can check the original diaries and other supporting documents there.

“The story, in a nutshell, starts with my ancestor, Sir Mervin Morgan. He was the first owner of this plantation. As a young man in the plantocracy, he was impressed upon by his family to marry a woman from a neighboring plantation, to forge his dynasty.

“It was not a love match. It was the practical thing to do. He chose Miss Anastacia Lowell as his bride. Her father’s plantation adjoined this one, and when I say adjoining, I mean a long distance from here. This was a large sugar plantation in the 1800s. The neighboring plantation was also large.”

Sir Reginald paused dramatically. “Now Lady Anastacia did not bear Sir Mervin an heir. They tried, but nothing happened.

“It was a great disappointment for the two of them, and after a year or two, their marriage became cold. Sir Mervin fell in love with one of his house slaves, Fabiola. Not to be outdone, Anastacia found herself enamored with the bookkeeper.

“The bookkeeper was a young gentleman named Nelson. He had flaming red hair and blue eyes. He knew it was wrong, he was a man of faith, but he fell for the lady of the house, and they had a torrid affair.

"An affair which completely missed Sir Mervin because he had had some drama of his own. He fell deeply in love with Fabiola.

Now, Fabiola was a seamstress, a mulatto, a skilled slave but still a slave and she was also personal maid to Lady Anastacia. She did not love Sir Mervin, she found him abhorrent. She was in love with a free black man named Samuel Jacobson.

"He was a visiting minister to this plantation where he preached to blacks and whites alike every Sunday. And he was smitten by the lovely Fabiola and she by him.

"Samuel asked Sir Mervin for Fabiola's hand in marriage, but Sir Mervin would not give his permission. He wanted Fabiola for himself.

"He was so in lust with Fabiola, it was the talk of the plantation. He didn't care that his wife knew, or anyone else for that matter. Sir Mervin wrote her poems and in general acted like a lovesick fool. Sir Mervin decided that he had to have her, and Fabiola had to resort to nefarious means to get him to leave her alone. In tandem with the house staff, a sympathetic lot, they spiked his drinks every night so that he would go to sleep early, and they alerted her if he was approaching her quarters in the days.

"It was an untenable situation as you could imagine."

The lady beside Tiana shifted in her chair and whispered. "Good lord poor Fabiola. I bet the cretin is going to get her."

Sir Reginald continued. "In the meantime, Rev Samuel was skating on thin ice. He was having secret meetings with freedom fighters on this plantation. Even though this plantation was not as bad as many others, as you can imagine, people just don't like to be caged and subjected to the will of others."

"Amen!" The lady beside her yelled.

That caused a chuckle that took a while to die down.

"But then Sir Mervin caught on to the plot to spike his drinks and Fabiola's role in it." Sir Reginald continued. "He became angry with her, and one day, he dragged her into his room and raped her."

"Sick monster. Somebody whispered."

Sir Reginald shrugged. "He regretted it. He was remorseful. Unfortunately, Fabiola became pregnant. Unbeknownst to Sir Mervin so was his wife, Lady Anastacia. Her assignation with the bookkeeper bore fruit.

"Both women had their babies on the same day. Fabiola had her son in the slave quarters below the kitchen and Lady Anastacia in the great house.

"Unfortunately for lady Anastacia, her baby looked like the bookkeeper. He was born with flaming red hair. As for Fabiola, her baby looked like Sir Mervin.

"When Sir Mervin found out all of this, he did something unheard of. He took Fabiola's baby and gave to Anastacia, and he took the ginger-haired baby and gave to the bookkeeper and banished him from the plantation.

"So Anastacia raised the son of a slave as her very own, they called him Reginald, my namesake. While her own child was taken away by his father. Rumor has it they returned to England and the child became a scientist. As for Fabiola, she was granted her freedom in exchange for her keeping the secret. She eventually married the reverend, the love of her life."

"Oh wow," Tiana found herself whispering. "I wonder how Anastacia felt about the whole scenario."

Sir Reginald heard and smiled at her. "I imagine she didn't like it one bit. I just gave you the bare bones of the story, the material is condensed from the diary of Lady Anastacia, the diary of Sir Mervin Morgan and the account of the butler who presided over the staff at the time. "

"What happened to Sir Mervin?" One of the writers asked.

"He lived until the age of sixty. His tombstone is in the church chapel."

"Did Sir Reginald discover that he was biracial in a racist plantocracy?" Tiana asked. "I can't imagine that his fake mother treated him well."

"He refers to her as his father's wife, never mother." Sir Reggie chuckled. "We can have a cup of tea and speculate about what transpired between them. However, it would only be speculation there are no records to verify how he felt."

"Okay." James stood up. "Thank you, Sir Reggie. You told that story well, as usual."

Sir Reggie smiled. "I will be at the bookkeeper's house for consultation if anyone is interested. You have an open invitation to visit and pick my brain about this place and the people that lived here."

James chuckled. "Where no doubt he will ply you with tea."

"I bid you adieu," Sir Reginald took a bow, "and good luck."

"You can start working on the pilot at any time," James said. "However tomorrow, from nine until three Jose and I will run through tips and tricks on how to write scripts for television."

"Tonight's dinner will be served on the patio. Everyone is invited. I know how writers get when you become engrossed in your scripts," Traci said. "It's our meet and greet and pick your brain time. You can meet me in the library for the keys to your accommodation. See you then."

Most people got up. Tiana still sat down her mind racing;

she was already seeing the story playing in her head. If done right, it would make a great biopic.

She was already imagining Fabiola as smart and sassy, and Anastacia, a product of her society, marrying the neighbor and unable to produce a child and then finding love with the bookkeeper.

And Mervin racked with guilt after raping the slave he claimed he loved.

"Tiana."

She dragged her mind from the story running in her head and focused on James' face. He was leaning close to her.

They had never voluntarily been this close before. She could see his stubby eyelashes and the mole above his lip, a subtle pinprick. On his blemish-free face, all his features were perfect and yet he wasn't pretty. He was the definition of uniquely handsome.

His father had to be spectacular because he did not look like his mother one bit.

"Do you want a tour of the house before you get settled in?" James asked, huskily.

Tiana blinked. She felt breathless as if she had run a marathon and she needed some air.

He was still leaning too close to her, and they were alone in the room. Everyone had left.

Her vocal cords had frozen, so she nodded instead.

James pulled back from the chair, and she breathed out in relief.

"I… er… thanks."

He didn't acknowledge that she was acting like a ninny. He nodded to the door. "Let's go, Princess."

She smiled. Princess. He called her Princess! Like the orchid. Was he telling her something?

"This is a fairly large house ballroom, tearoom, sewing

room, kitchen, it has two wings. Maybe I should show you to your accommodation so you can change into casual wear. Earlier the other writers were groaning by the time we finished the west wing."

"Oh, okay." Tiana nodded.

"We'll have lunch after you change. I am starving," James said, "and then we can get on with it."

They walked to what Tiana assumed was the library. It was a spacious place with a long conference table.

Traci was handing out keys at a desk, two persons were before her.

"Oh hey," she said when the two of them reached the desk. Tiana, you are rooming with Lesley Faraday." She held out a key. "Cottage 2."

"Like share a room?" Tiana blanched. "I have never shared a room with anyone."

James grinned when she said that. "How enlightening…"

"Don't worry," Traci said, "you won't be sharing rooms. The cottages are two and three bedrooms. You have a living room and a kitchenette and a glorious view of the great doors. You only have one housemate."

"Good," Tiana said in relief.

Traci nodded and opened her computer. "Excuse me, I have a ton of mail to attend to. My boss is popular."

James grinned.

Tiana looked up at a portrait above the conference room table. "Who is that?"

"The first Sir Reginald Morgan," James replied. "He was quite handsome, wasn't he?"

"Yes." Tiana nodded. "And now that I've heard his origin story, he feels more real to me. Do you have any more portraits of the major players in the story? I would love to visualize them."

"Sure thing." The sooner you get changed, the sooner you get your tour.

"Cool." Tiana looked back at Reginald the first. "I wonder what kind of slave master Reginald was, knowing that he was the son of a slave?"

"He was benevolent, his slaves were taught to read and write, and he paid wages long before abolition. Make no mistake; there was a reason this plantation was not involved in any slave revolts. And the reason why these buildings are in such incredibly great shape centuries later."

"Okay," Tiana said in relief, "I can now think about him sympathetically."

"Don't stray far from the task at hand," James warned. "We want a pilot. Starting with the key players, Mervin, Anastacia, and Fabiola, and maybe the bookkeeper, Reginald doesn't come into the picture until later."

"I know." Tiana nodded. "I won't stray. I was thinking that I could start with the courting of Mervin to Anastacia if there was courting," Tiana licked her lips, "and then show the wedding. And the slaves talking among themselves about the upcoming nuptials. And Fabiola as a young girl helping with the sewing. I am going to need the tour, see the sewing room."

James smiled. "You always had a fantastic imagination. I hope you do well, Tiana. Meet me back here in an hour. I'll be having lunch on the patio."

Tiana grinned. "I am beginning to get excited."

"I like when you are excited." James gave her a probing look. "That's just the way I remember you."

"I meant…" Tiana groaned. "Never mind."

Chapter Eleven

The cottages were arranged like a mini village. There was a novelty and gift shop at the very end of the bougainvillea lined road, and then there were the cottages. Each of them colorfully painted and built close to each other.

A post at the front of them displayed their numbers. Tiana parked in an empty graveled lot beside one of the houses and admired the view from where she stood.

Coconut trees dotted the landscape and beside cottage two was a loaded Julie mango tree.

A few of them were ripening. The air felt lighter and fresh, and she knew the back was going to have a view. She got a peek of it through the privacy fence on the other side.

It felt like paradise.

She dragged her suitcase to the tiny porch at the front and let herself inside. She paused when she opened the door. There was a glass door that opened to the most beautiful mountain views she had ever seen. The living room was spacious, and the place smelled a bit like potpourri. A tiny kitchen with a small island was off to one side, and then there were two doors which she assumed led to the bedrooms.

She left her suitcase in the hallway and walked to the opened patio.

"Hey, there, roomie." Lesley was lounging in a hammock with her laptop on top of her. "I took the liberty of taking the bedroom that has the mountain view," She grinned "because I was here first."

Tiana nodded. "No problem."

"I am Lesley Faraday by the way."

"Tiana Pryce," Tiana said, leaning on the rail and looking out. "This place is gorgeous and unspoiled. I imagine it looked just like this two hundred years ago."

"Oh, yes." Lesley nodded, "I was just soaking it in. I need to be one of three to stay here as long as possible. Besides, I need this vacation."

"What do you do?" Tiana asked.

"I am a teacher on vacation, mother of multiples, housewife," Lesley grinned, "and of course, secret writer."

"Multiples?" Tiana grinned. "I am a part of a triplet."

"You don't say." Leslie smiled. "I have twins." She laughed good-naturedly. "I love them, but I am enjoying the tranquility here. I hope you are not the chatty type, Tiana, because my ears need a break."

"Not at all." Tiana moved away from the rail, "I should go and get changed for my house tour."

Lesley nodded. "That James Dalton is fine. If I were single, I would be quietly losing my mind over him. As it is, I can barely look away when he is in the room."

Tiana chuckled. "Jose is not bad looking either. He looks like one of those heartthrobs in a telenovela.

"Jose, who?" Lesley asked dreamily. "There is no one

else around when there is James. I don't know why on earth Krista would have given him up. She was stupid if you ask me."

"You know Krista?" Tiana asked.

"Yes," Lesley nodded, "she is my coworker. She is a lovely lady."

"Okay," Tiana said unconvinced. "Krista seemed as if she would readily run her over with a truck if she got the chance."

Tiana left Lesley on the veranda and hurriedly went to her room, which was painted a cool mint color like the rest of the house. It had a king-sized bed. She sat on it to test its comfort and looked in the floor to ceiling mirror in front of her.

Her chignon was coming apart. She took out her hairpins and allowed her hair to fall to mid-back and then changed into jeans, a red shirt and matching flat wedges. She changed her bag to a tote and plopped her camera into it along with her voice recorder.

She was ready. She was getting hungry too. She hadn't eaten since breakfast, and though she was used to skipping breakfast, she would normally have had something to eat by now.

****

James was sitting on the patio as he said he would. He was sipping what looked like a broth and sifting through some papers.

"Sorry, Tiana," he looked up, "I couldn't wait to start lunch. It's buffet-style." He pointed to a sideboard with some sweet-smelling foods. "Dig in."

"Ooh." Tiana put down her bag and headed for the table. "The cottages are nice. If I weren't here to work, I could see myself spending my honeymoon there."

"Your honeymoon…" James looked at her sharply. "What is your fiancé like?"

"He is lovely," Tiana said abruptly.

James waited for her to say more. She didn't oblige.

"And when is the wedding?" James asked.

"We haven't set the date yet." Tiana sighed. "The engagement was recent."

"I hope he treats you with the love and respect you deserve and that your lives together will be happy," James said after a long pause.

"Thank you," Tiana cleared her throat, feeling like a fraud.

"So tell me about you," James said. "What have you been up to since high school?"

"Nothing special. I went to university, did English. Got myself a job at a publishing house. I sing in an award-winning youth choir, and I decided to start pottery last year. I am pretty good at it."

James narrowed his eyes at her. "Of all the things that I could have thought of Tiana the seductress doing, somehow I never imagined you as a church-going, pottery making youth choir singer."

"What did you envision me doing?"

James smiled. "What did I envision the girl who used to end all her essays with the line, to sir with love…mmm…"

"Don't say it," Tiana was resigned, "I changed my ways. You are the only one I stalked, wrote erotic literature to and basically made a fool of myself with. I told you, I grew up. After you, I was never a seductress again."

"What you felt for me was a normal part of growing up," James said gently. "You should have had taken all of that imagination and passion and put it into someone attainable. While I was your teacher, you were off-limits and vice versa."

"Did you even like me back just a teensy bit in high school?" Tiana asked huskily. She wanted to know, needed to know.

James took so long to respond, Tiana thought he wasn't going to.

"You made me uncomfortably aware of you," he finally said. "You were hard to ignore, Tiana. I made a valiant attempt though."

What did aware mean? Tiana wondered. Couldn't he be more specific?

"I have a confession." Tiana swallowed. "I was so drawn to you; it felt inevitable like when we met, this was it. I can't explain the certainty that I felt. Maybe that's why I was so persistent. The feeling was hard to shake, and I tried, I really did. I had this fantasy that it wasn't one-sided."

"I read your fantasies Tiana; I know what you thought." James sighed. "Let's just say it struck an answering chord, but I was the adult in our unequal relationship."

"You were just four years older. Hardly a huge age gap." Tiana pointed out. "You make it sound like you were so much older. You had just left college."

James grimaced. "I know, it still did not change my status as the one in authority. There is a reason why people are appalled when a teacher runs off with a student. Underage or not, age of consent or not, it is not professional or ethical. Besides, I was engaged to Krista at the time."

"She looks as if she hates me," Tiana murmured. "I am sorry if I broke you two up by my actions."

"Don't be." James shrugged. "It's ancient history. We've all moved on. Besides, you didn't break us up. We loved each other but obviously not ready for that type of commitment."

Tiana swallowed a jab of jealousy hitting her out of nowhere. He had loved Krista once. He probably still did now even though he claimed it was ancient history. Krista certainly didn't look at her as if she had moved on.

"So what did you do after you left teaching?" Tiana changed the subject; she didn't want to hear anything else about Krista; it made her jealous.

"I went to LA, got a job at a production house, learned it from the ground up, then started my own thing, with Uncle Reggie's help of course. I wrote the first couple seasons of secrets of love alone, and then I got help."

"Were you excited when you saw it on tv?" Tiana asked.

"Nervous." James admitted, "I didn't even want to watch it. And let me tell you it doesn't get easier with time. I have four shows on the burner now, all of them doing well."

"I know, that's amazing, congrats," Tiana said in a less than enthusiastic voice. "What do you spend your money on? Fast cars and even faster women."

She couldn't believe she said it out loud. She looked at him her eyes wide. "Don't answer that. It slipped out."

James laughed. "I am not into fast cars or women. I like commitment and stability. I want a love that can last a lifetime, like what my grandparents had. I haven't found her yet."

"Your mother wants you to settle down." Tiana took a sip of water; her throat was suddenly parched. "Maybe you and Krista can pick up where you left off." She struggled for nonchalance.

What on earth was she saying? Surely, she had gone crazy again. She was suggesting to James Dalton, the man that still made her weak like a newborn lamb, to pick up with his former fiancée. She was losing it.

James didn't say anything, which made her babble even more.

"You know she looks like my sister, Caroline?"

"Krista will be interested to hear that. She doesn't know anything about the Pryce side of her family." James leaned back in his chair. "When we were children, she was obsessed with finding her roots."

"You two knew each other as children?" Tiana asked jealously. There was no hiding it. She was swamped with the feeling. She was jealous of James Dalton's relationships and every female he was ever close to and especially Krista Pryce, the woman he had loved once and was engaged to and knew as a child.

She was becoming obsessed again. Elsa would be appalled to see her now. She could dismiss the past with the excuse that she was young and had a crush. What was she doing? What would she call this?

"Yes, I knew her. She was the girl next door," James said it softly as if he were seeing all the thoughts that were flying through her head.

"You don't have to worry about Krista. I will not treat her differently than I do the rest of you. She is competing for a spot to work for me and I don't want the perception that she will be given special treatment."

"Okay." Tiana reached for more water. That was not what she was worrying about, and luckily, James couldn't read her mind.

"It's quite a coincidence though… that we are all here like this." James mused. "It is a second chance for us to get things right this time around."

"A second chance," Tiana said determinedly. "I can show that I have matured, and you and Krista can pick up where you left off. Maybe you are destined to be with a Pryce after all."

"Maybe." James looked at her for so long she was beginning to feel warm. "We need to take that tour now. I don't want you to lag behind the others with your script writing."

Chapter Twelve

James watched while Tiana flitted through the rooms and took pictures and asked him questions. She was enthusiastic over the history, and she pretty much ignored him as she sat on beds looked through closets and stared through windows.

They were in Sir Mervin's room, and she was standing there, staring at Sir Mervin's portrait, while he stared at her. She still had him bothered, and obviously, he bothered her. He wasn't blind, and he could feel it. They still threw sparks off each other like before. Maybe they were destined to always feel that way about each other.

And maybe they were destined to always be in an unequal position with each other. Before he was her teacher, now he was going to judge her writing against other competitors. Before he was engaged to Krista, now she was engaged to Cole.

To everything, there was a season. The Ecclesiastes text popped up in his head. Maybe there would never be a season for them. The thought was depressing.

“Merv does not look like a perv," Tiana said after a while.

“No, he doesn't," James said. “He was probably just driven mad with unrequited love or lust, depends on who you talk to. You should read some of the poems he wrote to Fabiola, they are in his diary. One of his poems said I am the one that is enslaved, enslaved to your love. If I had the choice to set you free, I would forever keep you ensnared to me.”

“It sounds familiar, like something I would have written to you back in my obsessed moments.” Tiana murmured.

James looked at her sharply.

“Such a shame,” Tiana changed the subject, “all of these people were not perfectly matched, and they couldn’t do a thing about it.”

“True,” James murmured, “Anastacia and the bookkeeper, Mervin and Fabiola, Fabiola and Samuel…”

Tiana and James, he thought but didn’t say out loud. She was engaged to Cole. Every passing moment in her presence highlighted how much he resented that fact.

“At least Fabiola got a happy ending. She got to be with Samuel.” Tiana cut into his thoughts. “But then again, how happy could she be knowing that her son was being raised by Lady Anastacia? Have you ever thought that maybe it was not an easy decision for her to leave the boy with his father and the wife?”

James nodded. “I am sure it wasn’t, but she probably didn’t have much of a choice. She was a slave; children were the property of the master anyway. Those were different times.”

“Mmph.” Tiana muttered, “I wish she had diaries. I would read them. I bet they would have been more interesting than the others.”

“And Lady Anastacia, what went through her head when her husband snatched her child and sent him away with her lover, a man she must have had solid feelings for."

"She wrote in her diary that she was overcome with despair," James said, they both stopped in front of Anastacia's portrait, a smaller one than was in the gallery.

"She looked sad." Tiana said. "The artist got that accurately at least."

"How does it feel to be engaged to an artist?" James changed the subject abruptly, "Do you pose for him all the time?"

"That's so off-topic." Tiana looked at James. "I don't pose for him actually. He is more into landscapes than portraits. The painting your mother has of me is actually a picture from my sister Giselle's wedding. Cole saw it and decided to paint it. He said putting it in oil would make it better. He sold it fast. I didn't expect him to actually sell it, he claimed it was his favorite."

"I will say Cole Carr does have talent. That portrait of you was classic Tiana. He captured your personality perfectly."

"What do you mean my personality?" Tiana asked breathlessly. "I don't have any personality. I am bland and repressed."

James laughed out loud. "Tiana, you are the opposite of repressed. You are bright and refreshing and determined and persistent, and you speak your mind eloquently, and you throw yourself into the thing you love with passionate abandon. You love fiercely, and you are not afraid to show it."

"You should leave Cole if he is turning you into the opposite of that, life is too short."

Tiana stared at James with her eyes wide. "You…how do you do that?"

"What?" James asked.

"Read me so well." Tiana croaked. "It's like you…how do

you do it?"

"I am a people watcher, it's a hazard of the profession." James shrugged, "I observed you for two years when you were a teenager, you bathed me liberally with your thoughts. Without your defenses up I got some insight into the real you.

"In my opinion, the core personality is quite hard to change unless you were brain damaged or otherwise mentally compromised.

"Some of your enthusiasm for life and your empathy could have hardened over the years, but somehow, I am not sensing that in you. You'll make a great writer someday. Keep that empathy alive. Live passionately and don't let life make you jaded. Don't change that about yourself."

Tiana cleared her throat. "Wow. I just remembered that you used to give us little pep talks all the time."

"You just remembered?" James chuckled. "I am amazed you heard anything I said. You always seemed to be a bit spaced out around me."

"That is true," Tiana smiled sheepishly, "but I heard everything you said."

"If you are finished here, we have a lot more dour-faced Morgans to look at in the gallery and then on to Sir Reggie for a copy of the Morgan back story." James glanced at her; she looked pensive.

Had she really suppressed herself through the years and become a shadow of the person that she was? That would have been a shame. Tiana had always managed to effortlessly light up a room.

He wanted her to do well now. He wouldn't mind working with her on this project through to the end. It would certainly make every day something to look forward to.

"I wish Fabiola had a diary," Tiana murmured. "Do you

know if she was able to read or write?"

"No, I guess not," James said, "but Sir Mervin had a butler who wrote about the time he served here. He was here up until the first Sir Reginald was around fifteen years old. Uncle Reggie recently found his writings hidden under the floorboards of the butler's room when they were refurbishing. It was mostly about his duties and wine menus and other varied butlery things. He is in the process of decoding the manuscripts."

"What was his name?" Tiana mused. "Was he here with Sir Mervin from the beginning, before Anastacia came on the scene?"

"One volume is not translated yet, and I am not sure of his name," James responded.

"Can I read it?" Tiana asked.

"You read French?" James raised an eyebrow.

"And Spanish," Tiana grinned, "and I have more than a working knowledge of Mandarin."

"Impressive," James murmured, "they strolled through the gallery and then stopped at one particular painting."

"Who is this?" Tiana touched the frame and then stood back.

"The first Reginald's wife, Lady Eliza." James stood beside her. "She was a captain's daughter. It was said she posed as a male when she accompanied her father in his jaunts around the world. She met Reginald at the dock near here. The spark was instant. He wanted her to stay, and she decided her days of adventure were over."

Tiana smiled. "Good for Reginald. Did they live happily ever after?"

"No." James grimaced. "She and the child died in childbirth at twenty-one. At least they had four years together, and then he mourned a long while, and the burden of inheritance weighed on him, and he remarried a titled lady named Primrose, a pleasant woman by all accounts. She bore him three healthy sons."

"So sad," Tiana murmured.

"It's a mixed bag." James showed her to Anastacia's room. "He found happiness after a while. If it weren't for Primrose, the lineage would have died with Eliza, and my mother wouldn't be here. I wouldn't be here."

Tiana smiled weakly. "I see where you are going with this. I guess I am happy about him and Primrose because who wouldn't want you to be here? If you weren't here, the latter part of my teenage years would have been boring."

And my teaching days would have lacked some luster too. James added silently, but he couldn't tell Tiana that.

She was off-limits again.

He watched her as she smiled and asked questions and acted like she was at ease with him. He envied her casualness. There was a low humming tension between them despite their unspoken decision to ignore it. In the past he had repressed it by keeping his distance. Now he had to be in close proximity to her.

"Why is it that some people are drawn to each other, even though it is wrong or forbidden?" Tiana turned to him.

"Pardon?" James asked, huskily.

"I mean it's a theme throughout the Morgan family." Tiana slowed down and looked at one of his ancestors in the hallway. "Nobody loved who they were supposed to love and be attracted to. Do you have any ancestors who had a normal relationship?"

"Not on the Morgan side of the family," James mused. "My father's parents loved each other and were committed to each other for most of their life. When my grandfather died, my nonna said there was no one to replace him, and she wouldn't even try."

Tiana exhaled. "At least there is one committed couple in your family as an example for you."

"True," James looked at her, "And what about you? How did growing up an orphan with a brother who loves the ladies, how did that affect you?"

"You know about Toddy?" Tiana smiled.

"I may have overheard a conversation or two about it back in the day when I was your teacher." James shrugged. "Then there was the big divorce from that famous journalist, Celine Magnus, all the papers gleefully carried the story and highlighted his lifestyle. I remember wondering if that gave you some weird view on relationships."

"Maybe." Tiana grimaced. "I think in his own misguided way Toddy wanted us to have a mother, so he got married ever so often to supply us with one. I grew up with loads of examples of good relationships, despite Toddy. Even my sister Giselle. She married the love of her life. She has her career, and he has a growing business, and they have a toddler. They make it work."

"So is Cole the love of your life?" James asked. "I assume that is why you changed for him?"

Tiana looked at him and then looked away, a guilty look in her eyes. "I… er…about that…" she licked her lips.

"You shouldn't have to change for anyone," James said softly, "unless of course, it is a change for the better, and it is a relationship worth fighting for."

"Why didn't you fight for your relationship with Krista when you two were engaged?"

They were standing in the gallery landing, looking at each other intently. For the life of him, James wanted to sidestep the question. It wasn't something that he bothered to examine too closely even when it had happened, and the reason why he hadn't bothered to fight had a lot to do with Tiana.

He had felt the pull towards her then, and he knew to continue with Krista would have been a mistake.

And he was feeling it now. No woman since her had that effect on him. He had never felt this, whatever it was, with anyone else

"I was distracted at the time." He finally answered. "We should make our way to Sir Reggie's place if you want to see those manuscripts and get a move on."

"Yes." Tiana gave him one last probing look as if she didn't quite know what to make of his statement.

He schooled his expression into one of normalcy, but inside he was feeling conflicted about her again.

Chapter Thirteen

The bookkeeper's house was a three-bedroom stone house which was nowhere as fancy as the great house. It had a substantial wrap-around veranda. Sir Reggie was sitting at a round table having tea with Krista Pryce.

Tiana's heart sunk.

"The young lady with the theories!" Sir Reggie greeted her warmly when they approached the walkway.

"I feel like a king holding court today, I was visited by everyone today for the back story. You, Tiana, are the last of the lot. Come have a seat. You and my nephew are in for a treat. My interpreter just gave me a bit of new information from the butler's manuscript. It's interesting stuff."

"Really?" James sat down beside his uncle, forcing Tiana to sit beside Krista.

"It's remarkable how similar your eye color is to Krista." Sir Reggie looked between Tiana and Krista. "Same surname same eye color...a mystery in the making."

Krista looked at Tiana dismissively. "It could mean nothing."

"Well, well…" Sir Reggie steepled his fingers and looked from one girl to the other, "Krista here occasionally hounds me to investigate who her father is. I never made headway with that request, I had absolutely no idea where to start. I think this is a start, don't you think Krista?"

"You were telling us about the butler's manuscript," Krista interjected. "As much as I would like to explore my family ties I really want to get started."

She glared at Tiana. "Some of us are focused on the task at hand rather than other things like getting the man who we never got the chance to be with. Did you really stalk James like a cat in heat?"

Tiana flinched.

"The butler's manuscripts," Sir Reggie said calmly. "My translator found out a thing or two we would otherwise have missed in the other manuscripts. The butler was Fabiola's guardian. They were both from Haiti. They escaped during the revolution."

"The last manuscript is not yet translated. I told him to hurry; it could be important for the script."

"Can I see it?" Tiana asked. "Is it long?"

"Yes, you can see it," Sir Reggie said solemnly. "No it's not long. You do know it is in French. As I said, he was Haitian. A free man, not a slave. He served in the Haitian royal family. Can you read French?"

"Yes." Tiana nodded. "How long is the last volume?

"About sixty pages. I scanned them so you can get a soft copy now."

"I would be faster than your translator." Tiana rubbed her hands together.

"Sure." Sir Reggie got up. "I do hope you find something

usable."

He went inside leaving Tiana between James and Krista.

"Tiana Pryce." Krista turned to Tiana. "You broke up my relationship, you messed with my future."

"Krista!" James said sharply. "Stop it!"

"I am sorry," Krista growled back. "I just have to say what is on my mind. I just can't believe that she is here now. Why was she shortlisted? You can't have forgotten that she was the loony who pursued you like a rabid, hungry monkey, nearly ruining your life and reputation in the process. There should be no second chances for her."

"Traci shortlisted the writers. I had nothing to do with it. Tiana went through the vetting system you didn't," James said solemnly. "You are here purely because of our past connection."

He stressed past.

Tiana gave Krista a half-smile when James said that.

"And I really do not want any trouble, Krista," James continued. "This is not a dating show with me as some prize. If you cannot act professionally, I will ask you to leave."

"Me?" Krista widened her eyes. "I didn't do anything. I am just speaking my mind about Tiana Pryce who probably thinks she can coast by in life by being pretty. She probably can't write anything else, but the nonsense drivel she used to write in her high school English class, ending all her essays with to sir with love and attaching pictures to her essays in skimpy clothing as if that would get her a better grade."

"I grew up from that," Tiana said calmly. "And frankly you don't know anything about me now."

"Oh I do," Krista shook her head. "Your writing then was amateur at best. I am almost sure it hasn't gotten any better in six years. I know your type. You coast by on your looks and your connections. If there is any fairness in this world, you are going to be eliminated soon, and I can breathe easier without having to look at your desperate, pathetic face."

Tiana gasped. It stung. She didn't coast by with anything in her life. And Krista's attack was grossly unfair since she was the one who was there because of her connections. She swallowed her anger and projected a calm she wasn't feeling.

Elsa's voice rung in her head, be mature and professional. Tiana turned to Krista, no emotion on her face.

"That was a whole lot of pent up hate for something that happened years ago, haven't you moved on with your life at all? Because I have. I even have a whole fiancé, and I have written a lot more things since high school English class."

James smiled, faintly at that.

Krista subsided in her chair, "Oh well... I apologize."

"Apology accepted," Tiana said in the same tone. "Let's just move on."

"Two feisty women with the same surname." Sir Reggie walked onto the veranda. "I am very much looking forward to both of your scripts."

He handed Tiana the jump drive. "If you find anything interesting, come and tell me about them. I don't mind the details, however inane."

Tiana nodded. "Yes, Sir." She got up, "I should get started."

She nodded in their general direction and walked briskly in the direction of the cottage.

****

Reggie chuckled when Tiana was out of sight. "Lovely woman reminds me of Grace, my first wife. Feisty and pretty, talented and smart in the same package. Oh, how I loved that woman. I didn't know what I was going to get from one day to the next. She could hold her own in any situation. A wise man holds on to a woman like that. Except I didn't."

James grimaced. "I think her fiancé would appreciate that advice."

He turned to Krista. "What got into you? You attacked her without provocation."

"The two of you came strolling by, and I lost it." Krista shrugged, "I got a little jealous."

"But you have no right to be jealous," James hissed. "We have not seen or spoken to each other in years. There is a whole lot of living between then and now."

"You always end up defending her, don't you?" Krista said crossly. "You can't help yourself. You liked her in high school, and you like her now. I bet it bothers you that she is engaged. I didn't break up with you six years ago because I thought you had a physical connection with your student.

"I broke up with you because from the moment you met her, things changed with us. Even the blind could see it then, James! You have always had an emotional thing for Tiana Pryce! Maybe just as much as she had a thing for you."

Sir Reggie cleared his throat. "Well, Krista…"

"Tell him to deny it!" Krista yelled, "ask him if he is not already plotting how he can break up her engagement so that they can finally be together. I am sure that this voting process will not be equitable."

James narrowed his gaze at Krista. "The final say as to which script gets the nod will be among four people, Jose, Traci, Sir Reggie and myself. I fail to see how I can tip the scales in Tiana's favor. You are treading on thin ice, Krista. I don't like what you are implying. Maybe you should leave now. Take some time to cool off before I forget that we were once friends."

Krista's face crumpled. "I am sorry. I have no idea what came over me. You are right. This is ancient history, and I really want to be a part of this project."

She got up. "I am so sorry, Sir Reggie, James…"

She left the veranda a slump to her shoulders.

"What a dramatic start to the production." Sir Reggie turned to James. "The two Pryce women in your past are back for round two. How on earth did you manage this screw-up?"

"It's all unintentional. I said yes to Krista before I even knew Tiana was on the shortlist." James shrugged. "And now Tiana is here, and Krista is short-circuiting like we broke up just yesterday."

"I'll further talk to Krista." Reginald frowned. "She is so consumed by her hatred of Tiana she hasn't even realized that this is a golden opportunity to sort out the mystery of her Pryce family tree. The fact that they have the same last name and eye color is suggestive."

"And you love a good mystery," James murmured.

"I do." Sir Reggie nodded. "She is my godchild. She asked me to find her father's family, and I have failed."

"An impossible task," James said, "when you have nothing to go on."

"True." Reggie nodded, "but I now have a lead. Tiana Pryce is my lead."

James frowned at Reggie. "Can I count on you not to favor either of them in this writing interview? I know you have a soft spot for Krista, you financed her schooling, and I know you want Tiana around because you want to solve your mystery, but I need the best writing team around me for this project. Your emotions should not be allowed to sway you."

"Of course, nephew," Sir Reggie said solemnly. "The question is, how did I become embroiled in a pep talk meant for yourself."

Chapter Fourteen

Tiana looked at the screen in dismay. Sir Reggie had told her the document was around a sixty pages, he didn't t say it was single-spaced and written in Haitian Creole.

Haitian Creole and French were a little different, especially with the meaning of some words. This project would eat into her time. She could almost see herself lagging behind the rest of the writers as they focused on the task at hand while she sifted through this butler's experience and probably ended up with nothing new.

She made a valiant effort to start. Lesley, her housemate, had passed her several times to go into the kitchenette. She was sipping some water and looking at Tiana speculatively. "What are you reading? Anastacia's diary?"

"No, just some material from the butler who was here in Sir Mervin's time. The writing is in Creole."

"Really now?" Lesley moved closer. "What did you find?"

"Nothing important yet." Tiana sighed. "He is writing

about his origin story. It says, 'My name is Michel Olivier. My mother was the concubine of an aristocrat. I, her only surviving offspring, was educated along with my legitimate siblings and then I left my father's household to work as head butler for Duc Perrier.

"'Duc Perrier had property in the colony Saint-Domingue. I had a feel for adventure one year, and I accompanied him on his journey to the tropics. He spoke so highly of the place, its beauty its uniqueness, I was lured from the comfort of my comfortable job as a domestic in Paris.

"'I never regretted my choice until I was caught in the intrigue of the island of Saint Domingue and in the middle of a love tryst of the Duc's household. His daughter Carmen was with child for one of her slave boys. She didn't know which. Miss Carmen had what the ladies would delicately call jungle fever. Her father's many male slaves were her playthings.

"'I must admit there is a soft spot in my heart for Miss Carmen despite her promiscuous nature. When the duchess died, she was allowed to run wild without much supervision. Unfortunately, for me, it was that soft spot for the lady that made me bid adieu to my beloved Paris. Miss Carmen had the baby in secret and then bid her nurse and me to take her and protect her, to treat her as if she was ours. You see, Lady Carmen was betrothed to marry an earl and she had to leave for France before she could do so.

"'Harriet and I were left in the colonies to care for the girl child she called Fabiola.'"

"That's downright interesting." Lesley sat on the settee. "So Fabiola was the illegitimate child of a duchess and her slave lover?"

"Yup." Tiana nodded.

"Read more." Lesley urged.

"Well, he talks a lot about the uprising in Haiti. The slaves burned down the great house where he was living, and he fled with Fabiola and Harriet to a small house near the dock where his friends lived. There he met an English nobleman who was moving to his new house in Jamaica, Michel asked him to be his butler. He told him that he came with Harriet a skilled seamstress and their charge, a little girl by the name Fabiola.

"That English man was Mervin Morgan, and he agreed to the arrangement."

Tiana rubbed her eyes.

"Go on," Lesley murmured. "It sounds as if you are getting to the good part."

"But how would it fit into the pilot, though." Tiana frowned. "This is the background for Fabiola, but do we have space for this in the pilot?"

"No, but it is good to know." Lesley mused. "It's like getting all the facts before you start writing, you can keep it at the back of your mind in case you want to incorporate it in later episodes."

Tiana nodded. She skimmed through a few pages, Michel Olivier was meticulous with his descriptions of the great house and the furnishings in the house down to the minutest details. That information would be important for the wardrobe and the set.

And then she saw mention of Sir Mervin Morgan and Fabiola.

"Here's something," she read out loud. "'At sixteen, Fabiola has grown into a fine young woman, and she has caught the master's eye. The mistress is aware of this but alas she is occupied elsewhere.

"'I would have preferred a better match for Fabiola than to be the concubine of the master, a marriage perhaps. Maybe a titled landowner of some sort but I have no clout, and Lady Carmen has abandoned her child as if she was never born.

"'I cannot arrange beneficial marriages for Fabiola. This island is more rigid in their class system than France or even Saint Domingue. Harriet has taught her how to sew, and she is an excellent seamstress. She is somewhat renowned for her prowess with the needle in these parts.

"'My only sore point with Fabiola is her unhealthy fascination with the Baptist preacher, Samuel Jacobson. Sir Mervin would never allow their union. He wants Fabiola for himself. I have never seen a more lovesick man in my life.

"'This is a house of intrigue. Sir Mervin is in love with Fabiola. Lady Anastacia is in a torrid affair with the bookkeeper, Nelson Barnaby, a man who has a rather inflated view of himself. The master has no idea that lady Anastacia spends most of her time in the bookkeeper's residence under one pretext or the other. He is too busy pursuing Fabiola like a lovelorn fool.

"'Even Harriet is in on the intrigue. She is trying to quell Sir Mervin's libido with a concoction of chaste berry, licorice, hops, and wild lettuce and excess drinks at dinner. Harriet wants a different future for Fabiola as I do.

"We are not pleased with Jacobson, the preacher, but we do not want the master for our precious girl…'"

"That's juicy." Lesley snapped her fingers. "That's good stuff. That's detailed stuff. You shouldn't tell anyone else. Let them find out after they write the pilot. We have gold here."

Tiana looked at her aghast. "No Lesley, I think we should share what we know."

"This is a competition Tiana," Lesley said exasperated. "The only advantage you have is information, little nuggets of delicious information that will turn the tides. It's the survival of the fittest. Don't tell them a thing."

Tiana regarded Lesley's animated face. I promised Sir Reggie that I would tell him if I found anything. He'll be at the dinner tonight. We should get ready."

"Nah, not interested in the dinner." Lesley shook her head. "Too many precious hours to lose. I am here to work not to socialize. I know what I am going to do now, which angle I am going to take, thanks to you."

Lesley stood up. "I can't wait to write."

Tiana watched her as she headed for her room and then got up. She took her time to shower. She didn't bother to use her own soap; the cottage had lemongrass, soaps, and shampoos. It felt and smelled wonderful.

She changed into a simple khaki shift dress with palm leaves at the side and put on matching comfortable khaki wedges. She would walk to the great house, not drive. To drive would be overkill and it was a nice evening out.

When she stepped out there was a light drizzle, but the evening sun was still out. It didn't look like it was going to rain any harder and she could barely feel the raindrops anyway.

The walk to the great house took longer than she had anticipated. She stopped at every interesting tree and view and photographed it.

There was a stone bench under a huge blossoming poui tree, and she sat on it. Not because she was tired but because she wanted to think. She could see the great house in the distance glowing in the evening sun. She closed her eyes and thought about how it would look in 1804.

The whole place was probably buzzing with industry. It was the height of the sugar trade after all, and this was one of the largest sugar plantations in Jamaica in its heyday. She thought about the hierarchy on a typical plantation. At the top was the owner, Mervin Morgan, then below him was the manager.

There had to have been a manager, large plantations usually had one. She wondered who that had been.

And then there were the overseers and the bookkeepers; they were usually white men. And then there were skilled craftsmen, the carpenters, coopers, blacksmiths, potters, sugar boilers, they were usually black.

The lighter-skinned slaves, often the children of the owner or manager by a slave woman, were often given the better jobs, kept as house servants or trained in a skilled job.

Like being a seamstress.

Fabiola was the result of such a union. What had happened to her mother, Carmen?

It was clear now why her son could pass for white.

Fabiola was an integral part of the narrative. Tiana thought. This should be her story, or it could be the story of the French butler, seeing the workings of the plantation through his eyes, like a narrator.

"Hey there." A friendly voice jerked Tiana out of her contemplation. "Are you on your way to dinner?"

It was one of the few male writers. He was tall, and chunky. He sported long locks and had kind eyes. He had one of those faces that made her feel like giving him a hug. Tiana had forgotten his name. "Hey, er…"

"Lincoln Gold." He chuckled and walked over to her and sat down. "I don't remember your name either."

"Tiana Pryce." She smiled at him.

"Tiana," he smiled, "lovely name, I shouldn't forget it again. My wife's name is Giana. So why are you wistfully staring at the great house?

"You are not hoping to see a glimpse in time, are you? Is this the spot for it?"

Tiana laughed, "No. I am just exercising my imagination. I just read an excerpt from the butler's diary, the one who came back from Haiti with Sir Mervin. I was allowing my imagination to run wild."

"Tell me more." Lincoln looked at her excitedly. "Was there additional juicy information?"

"In a manner of speaking," Tiana said, "the diaries gave a lot more background on Fabiola and others."

****

Tiana was a little late for dinner after talking to Lincoln, about the butler's diary. She realized that he had a fascinating and creative mind, and he knew a wealth of history about eighteenth-century Jamaica, and a million and one ideas that she hadn't even thought of. She was glad they got the opportunity to chat.

When they approached the great house, the patio lights were already on. They were round white lanterns that gave the space a festive air.

It seemed as if everybody was out except for Lesley and Krista.

No Krista. It felt like physical relief.

"I am going to monopolize Sir Reginald," Lincoln said, "I think he might come up with something I can use. Thank you for sharing your findings with me Tiana. I hope we end up in the top three."

Tiana nodded. She hoped so too. She liked his easy-going personality.

James spotted her as soon as she entered the patio area and walked over. He had changed his clothes from earlier. He was in a white shirt folded up his arms and tucked into blue jeans. He was freshly shaven. He had tried to brush back his curly hair off his face. It hadn't quite worked.

He looked healthy and fresh and handsome. When he approached, she felt her knees getting a little weak.

"Hey." He walked up to her. "You came."

"I found out some things from the butler's script." Her voice was whispery. She cleared her throat. "It was très intéressant."

"Very interesting?" James raised a brow.

"Oui." Tiana nodded. She found herself staring at him, his hard jaw, the curve of his lips. They looked pinker than usual.

"Tiana," James moved closer to her, "you stopped speaking English."

"Sorry," she laughed shakily, "I might not be hungry. Maybe I should go, there is a piece more of the document I am yet to go through."

"Stay." James came even closer; she could sniff his aftershave. "I am sitting over there with Traci and Jose, take a plate and come join us. We'd love to hear about the butler's account."

Tiana stood dazed. Something about the aftershave triggered a memory. The first time she had kissed him, planted her lips on his and forced her tongue in his mouth…

"Tiana," James said to her, huskily, "what's wrong?"

"Nothing," Tiana said brightly, too bright.

She needed to get a grip. She followed him to the table with Jose and Traci, smiled and chatted told them what she had read. She eventually told the other writers too.

She was the center of attention, answering questions about Michel Olivier and his adventures with Fabiola.

She was feeling weary by the time nine o'clock rolled around. Some of the writers had already left.

"I have to go," she whispered to James, "I am going to

crash."

"Let me walk you home." James stood up. He held out his hand to her, and she took it.

"I might fall asleep on my feet." She yawned widely.

"I'll catch you," James grinned, "and throw you over my back and carry you to the cottage." Traci and Jose laughed. Tiana blinked at him rapidly. She could imagine him doing that, and she would like it.

"I walk in the mornings at five," James said when they were on their way. "I might be walking past the cottages at around five-fifteen."

Tiana looked at him sleepily. "Is that an invitation to walk with you?"

"No." James shrugged. "I wouldn't mind the company though. I find that walking stimulates creativity."

"You are on," Tiana murmured. "It's a good thing I carried my walking clothes and shoes and headband and…"

James took her hand and stopped her. She faltered; her whole body trembled.

"Listen, Tiana." He pulled her around to face him, and she turned as if her bones were made of fluid.

"This is long overdue," James whispered near her lips. "I think we should get this out of the way. We'll be more comfortable around each other, I think. Just this one time. Destroy the tension."

Tiana's heart thudded heavily in her chest, she nodded. "Okay."

James chuckled. "Just okay, after eight years of build-up? That's all you have to say?"

"I can't think when you are so close." Tiana moved in even closer to him.

He fished one hand in her hair, and brought his lips to hers, while his other hand cupped her bottom and brought her so close to him that she could feel his heart beating against hers. They both moaned together, as the kiss got deeper and then her arms were around his neck, and she was kissing him back as hungrily as he was kissing her... she took over the kiss.

It was the sound of laughter in the distance that broke them apart. James heard it before Tiana.

Tiana gazed at him; her eyes wide. “Just this one time you said?”

“Yes,” James placed his forehead on hers. “You have a fiancé.”

“There is that.” Tiana sighed. “This job interview was for me to see if I still felt anything for you. It was supposed to settle my emotions, see if they were real. I would get you out of my system, and I would move on with Cole. At least that’s what I promised to Yara.”

“How is that working out for you?” James asked his eyes serious.

“Not well.” Tiana’s voice was shaky. She stepped back from him when they heard footsteps getting closer.

“I’ll walk you to your cottage.” James’ voice wasn’t quite steady either.

He put some distance between them and walked her to her door. “Don’t work too hard. He touched her cheek and stepped back. Goodnight Princess.”

“Goodnight, James.”

She turned to the door, opened it, and leaned on the wall with her heart racing a million miles a minute.

She didn't want to overthink what just happened or do a postmortem on it, she just wanted to relive it over and over. She would not sleep a wink tonight. Her whole body was on high alert. She needed a shower, a cold one.

Chapter Fifteen

Tiana put on her jogging shoes and stepped outside. It was five-fifteen a.m. The streetlights were still on. There was a cat curled up in one of the patio chairs. He looked up at her lazily, fit himself into a tighter ball and went back to sleep. There was a slight drizzle, but nothing was going to stop her from taking this walk with James Dalton. She still couldn't believe they actually kissed. She was probably still at home in Kingston, and this was an elaborate dream she was experiencing.

It felt real enough, though, and she didn't want it to end. So she was going to endure the light rainfall, and she was going to walk with James. They were going to stop at some convenient romantic spot, and he was going to declare his undying love…

She stopped mid-thought when she saw two figures heading her way. She knew James' gait, but the other person was…Krista!

Tiana groaned inwardly. Krista Pryce. Fantasy over.

She had somehow completely dismissed Krista from her mind, though it was only yesterday that Krista had managed to completely denigrate her and her writing skills. She had called her desperate and pathetic and amateur. It seemed so long ago now.

Tiana considered going back inside, what was Krista doing out here anyway? Why was she walking with James?

"Don't leave!" Krista called, her voice sounding uncharacteristically humble.

Tiana turned with her hand on the door.

"I was on my way to see you, and James was headed this way. What a coincidence, huh?" Krista said sarcastically.

"Now that was more like it," James said.

Tiana grimaced and looked at James.

"Good morning." She managed to say casually. "Seems as if we are all early risers."

"I have always been an early riser." Krista pushed her hand in her jacket pockets. "To be honest, I didn't sleep a wink last night. I was thinking about you."

"Me?" Tiana rubbed her eyes, "Why?"

"Because you said I looked like your sister Caroline, and it wouldn't leave my head."

"You acted like you didn't care." Tiana pointed out. "You shrugged it off."

"But I do care," Krista said sheepishly. "I care a lot. As you said, I was acting. James will tell you that I am on a quest to find my father's family. It is a little obsession of mine. My mother left me on the great house steps when I was three months old. She left a note to Sir Reggie saying that he was to watch out for me and a note to her sister, Beatrice, to take care of me."

"I see." Tiana inhaled, "can we walk and talk? I wanted

to see the church where the freedom fighters used to meet. I don't know how that will factor into my script."

"Sure, Krista glanced at James. "I guess you'll be coming to the church too, huh."

James nodded. "Why not?"

"You two arranged to meet here, didn't you?" Krista asked suspiciously.

"Not really." James shrugged. "I had no idea if Tiana would be up at this hour."

"But you were hopeful, though." Krista shook her head. "I knew this day would finally come, you are getting the right Pryce now aren't you, James? The one that you have always wanted, the pretty rich one."

Tiana looked at James to see his reaction, he glanced at her but didn't reply. "I like my morning walks to be stress-free, Krista."

"Hmm." Krista snorted.

"Why did you get the idea that I was rich?" Tiana asked puzzled. "This is the second time that you called me a rich girl."

"You went to Bellfield," Krista said, "only rich kids go there."

"You went to Mount Faith University," Tiana said, "does that make you rich?"

"Sir Reggie paid for my education." Krista shrugged, "He paid for a lot of us in the village, the ones who showed potential. I was bright he took an interest in my education, especially since he's my godfather."

"What happened to your mother?" Tiana asked.

"Drug overdose." Krista snapped, "She was a prostitute, one of those high-end ones, somebody got her hooked on drugs. She died before I was two."

Tiana gasped.

"See, I didn't have your smooth upbringing. I bet you had your doting parents and a family swimming with money. Friends galore and people who would do anything for you."

Tiana laughed dryly. "You are so wrong. Actually, my father died before I was born, my mother was killed by my aunt's boyfriend's wife. My sisters and I, the three of us, were left with no parents, and no adults to take us. All the adults on the Kennedy side of my family were wiped out at the same time. We were nearly three years old. And my father's side of the family, the Pryces, hated my mother and wanted nothing to do with us."

"Why did they hate your mother?" James was the one who asked. He had been listening keenly to her.

Tiana glanced at him. "My mother was forty-two years younger than my father. They thought she was a gold digger and therefore blamed her for his death. They thought she er…" Tiana grinned, "excited him too much in the bedroom."

James chuckled.

Krista had a smile on her face too, even though she looked like she didn't want to smile. "Could we really be related?" Krista asked. They passed the great house and took a side road that led to some other buildings.

"It's possible," Tiana said. "You have to be related somehow, your nose, eyes, the shape of your chin, the shade of your skin, it's all Pryce."

"Let me show you." She pulled out her phone, and the three of them stopped beneath the nearest streetlight. It was beginning to get light out anyhow.

Tiana scrolled through the phone and found a picture. She handed it to Krista. "This picture is unusual. All of Wilton Pryce's children in one place. I think this is the first time anything like this was happening."

Krista pored over the phone like a starving man being

shown water.

"Caroline had arranged for it to happen," Tiana continued. "She had finally been appointed high court judge and had bullied, begged, and otherwise pleaded for all her siblings to be there."

Tiana stretched while James and Krista examined the picture.

"Caroline is in the middle, in her judge robes," Tiana said. "As you can see, there are ten of us."

"All of you are brothers and sisters?" Krista whispered. "Goodness."

Tiana came over to them and pointed. "The oldest is Barrington." She pointed to her oldest brother. "He is a retired engineer, next up is Lovell, he is also retired, but he was a soldier and then became an inventor, and then that's Mary Jane she was a trauma nurse. She's now retired and lives in Florida, then there is Peter, tenured professor at Harvard, then Caroline the high court judge and Theodore affectionately known as Toddy, the senator and then there is Laila. She is a doctor. When she came to that event, it was my first time meeting her. She said she will never come to Jamaica ever again. I don't know why. Toddy said she suffered some trauma or something. You look more like her than Caroline actually."

"Yes, I do," Krista whispered.

"And who are these the rest of the girls that look like you?"

"That's Giselle, and that's Elsa. My sisters. We are triplets."

"Ah," Krista nodded, "I've seen Giselle on television before. You guys look different from the rest of your siblings."

Tiana took back her phone. "My mother was of Indian descent."

"That explains the hair," Krista muttered, "but you got the

Pryce eyes."

"The only one of the triplets to get it." Tiana shrugged. "The truth is Elsa and Giselle are almost identical, they could be twins, and then there is me. I look like them but clearly different."

"Yes, but not by much." Krista sighed, "so tell me about your father."

"As I said, he died before I was born," Tiana said. "I grew up with my brother Toddy."

"The senator?" Krista whispered. "Whose child out of all of them do you think I am? I am twenty-eight. I could be your father's child, couldn't I? What was his name?"

"Wilton Pryce," Tiana frowned, "you could be. He was alive at the time and hadn't married my mother yet."

"Did he have any brothers?"

"Yes," Tiana nodded, "but they are all dead. My father was the youngest, and he would have been in his seventies when we were born. As you can see, my oldest brother could be my grandfather. He has grandchildren my age."

"That's Barrington, right?" Krista raised her eyebrows. "What was he up to twenty-nine years ago?"

"He was in the States," Tiana said, "but who knows, maybe he visited Jamaica at the time. As I said, I don't really know them. They hated my mother, and by extension, they hated us or at least what we represented. It's only in recent years that most of them are even acknowledging that we exist."

"What about Lovell?" Krista asked as if she wasn't listening to all the information Tiana had given her.

"He lives in Canada," Tiana said dutifully. It was easy to feel sorry for Krista. She sounded so forlorn.

"And Peter?" Krista turned to her fully. "Tell me about him."

"He is a professor; he lives in the US and is married and

has two children. He is a grandfather too. He does visit Jamaica regularly. He has a house out here in Montego Bay. He comes out every summer."

"Does he take his wife?"

Tiana laughed, "I have no idea. I don't even know where the house is."

"Your family sounds less than close," Krista muttered.

"Except for Toddy and us."

"Mmm," Krista was silent, "could Toddy be my father?"

"It's not impossible," Tiana said, "but Toddy is a strong believer in taking care of his children, and he is heavily involved with his grandchildren too. He is the family-oriented one. He raised me and my sisters. There is no way he would have known about you and ignored you. Why don't you ask your Aunt Beatrice if your mother gave her any indication who her lover's baby was?"

"Aunt Beatrice does not know what my mother was up to when she left this place. She didn't even know about me until my mother dropped me off at the great house steps with the letters."

"Ah." Tiana nodded.

"So the only thing I know about my mother is what aunt B knows and I know how she looks because of some old dusty photos Aunt B has in an album. I look nothing like her."

"What was her name?" Tiana asked.

"Annessa Baylor," Krista said quickly.

"I'll talk to Toddy about this," Tiana said, "maybe he can help."

Krista nodded. "Thanks. Any help will be appreciated. I know I have not been particularly friendly to you, and you don't have to do this for me. It's quite odd how things work out. I was praying about finding my family for years, and there you were in the background pursuing my fiancé."

"Not that again," Tiana murmured.

"I saw your picture, the one you attached to the essay that you sent to James and I saw your eyes and I said, maybe we are related, but I never pursued it."

"It would have been a long shot," Tiana said, "unless you met me in person."

Krista nodded. "And that I didn't want to do. I was out of my mind with jealousy at the time."

"Over me?" Tiana squeaked.

"Yep," Krista smirked, "James is not perfect, you know. He might look perfect, but he is a man, which means he is flawed. He forgets that you are around when he is caught up in one of his scripts or busy with work. He'll forget your birthday and anniversaries. He doesn't cook or wash dishes, he talks in his sleep, and he is only marginally tidy. He has a couple good qualities though, he is an above par lover, quite surprising since he is handsome. They tend to be selfish in bed, but not James."

Tiana gasped.

"Thank you for that mixed review, Krista," James said sarcastically. "I am not sure why you had to tell Tiana any of that."

"Because I can see what's between the two of you." Krista smirked. "You can't fool anyone. You can both pretend, but it's there. I am sorry for your fiancé Tiana. I am going home."

She pointed downhill toward the village. "I guess I'll see you two later at the scriptwriting session."

"See you." James watched as she walked away and then turned to Tiana. "I swear I am much tidier now, and since I live alone, I had to learn how to cook. I still hate dirty dishes, so I let my dishwasher do all the work, and she is right I am not a selfish lover."

"Really now?" Tiana raised an eyebrow. "Do you miss

making love to her?"

"No." James sighed. "I moved on. There have been others since her, none in the past couple of months. I have been missing that emotional connection and decided to be celibate until I got it."

"Here comes the sunrise." James changed the subject, "How comes I never knew that you were an orphan at three."

Tiana smiled. "I never got the opportunity to tell you. We didn't have the kind of relationship where you would get to hear these things."

"Mmph," James grunted. "When you were in high school, you had daddy issues. Maybe that's why you liked me so much."

Tiana laughed, "Oh, hell no. I never had daddy issues, and you are too young for me to have daddy issues about. My boyfriend Cole is older than you."

James pulled her ponytail and grinned. "Maybe you had an authority figure fetish."

"Maybe." Tiana grinned, "but I've never been that way with anyone else, and trust me, I had plenty of handsome teachers at university."

James sobered up. "Tiana…"

"Yes, James." Tiana batted her eyes at him.

"I may as well come clean, I felt it too, I was just better at hiding my emotions." He sighed. "Everything has a season; our time together is not yet. Maybe we are two persons destined to run into each other when we are in different places in our lives, committed to other people. Maybe we'll meet again in a nursing home, me a slightly frail but still sharp ninety-year-old, you a spritely eight six without teeth and we'll finally get our time to be together."

Tiana laughed. "Why do I have to be without teeth?"

"It won't matter to me," James shrugged, "I'll be half-blind."

Tiana stopped and had a good laugh. "Okay then, it's curious you would quote that text, that was what Cole had the choir sing at the proposal."

"And you said yes." James stared at her. "You really want to marry him?"

"Well, I don't know. Everybody thinks we look good together though. He is a great guy, and we get along quite well. Maybe life is not supposed to be about fireworks and passion, those wear off."

"Does it really?" James murmured.

They stopped at the end of the pathway where the church was.

"I have been assessing things since last night."

"Since the kiss." James turned to her.

"And everything is so clear to me now. I want you sexually. I have always wanted you like that. Back in the days I was not afraid to let you and half the world know." Tiana sighed, "but friendship is better. That's something I have with Cole.

"I want the kind of love and friendship to last me a lifetime. Not a flare-up hot and heavy moment and then coldness in the end."

James whistled. "The Tiana Manifesto. What's wrong with having both passion and friendship. I heard it on good authority from my nonna that it is possible. Did you know I barely slept last night? That kiss had me worked up."

"I slept like a baby after taking a cold shower," Tiana murmured. "You should take more of those."

"I can do that." James kissed her on the forehead. "Well, friends it is, Tiana. I can be your friend. Since we both have the passion thing, all worked out."

Chapter Sixteen

Tiana was racing against time, days two and three had been easy. She had Michel Olivier, the butler's diary as a guide and she had the full picture in her head of what she wanted to do.

Her last few days had taken on the same pattern. She walked with James in the mornings, had breakfast with him, ran ideas by him and then wrote for the day. She met him for dinner, and then wrote in the nights. It was rinse and repeat after that.

Day four, found her in the great house library seeking some information from Anastacia's diary. Krista and Lesley were sitting in the furthest corner of the library, their heads bent together whispering.

If she had been tuned in, she would have realized that there was a whole other world taking place around her that she was not a part of.

"If you want copies of the diaries," Traci said to her when

she entered the room, "I have it on jump drive. I am on my way out, taking a trip with Jose and James to Anastacia's plantation. Jose is curious about footage."

"I wish I could tag along." Tiana grimaced, "but I have a lot of writing left to do."

"I am sure you'll get the chance to if you are chosen to be in the top six." Traci gave her a thumbs up, "I am rooting for you."

"Thank you." Tiana looked around. Lincoln was sitting at the other end of the room, from Lesley and Krista.

She headed to where he was sitting.

He looked up and smiled. "Hey, Tiana, I have been in here every day. Don't tell me this is your first time."

"Yup." Tiana nodded. "I had all the info that I wanted until now."

"How is it going?" Lincoln grinned. "You almost done?"

"No, maybe." Tiana shrugged. "I know what I want the title to be. I feel a little nervous that I am going in a very different direction from everyone."

"Thinking outside the box will make your work stand out." Lincoln leaned back in his chair.

There was a burst of laughter at the other side of the room. Tiana looked across and her eyes met Krista's.

"Sorry," Krista said, "Lesley is a hoot."

Tiana nodded and then turned to Lincoln, "I have not seen Lesley in a while, and she's my housemate. I assumed that she was in her room writing!"

"She's always in here pacing the floors, I don't think she has written anything much." Lincoln lowered his voice. "I think she is panicking. So which direction have you taken this?"

"I am doing this from the butler's viewpoint, so I am starting with the dock scene when he met Merv in Haiti when he and Henrietta were fleeing the revolution with a young Fabiola.

"I can envision them arriving in Jamaica and going up the driveway in a horse-drawn carriage. I want the butler to be a narrator."

"Ah, that's a good idea." Lincoln snapped his fingers. "Very good."

"What did you end up with?" Tiana smiled at him and opened her laptop.

"I thought of telling the story backward," Lincoln said, "like giving snippets of the past in the present and then build on the story."

"I'd love to see how you handle that." Tiana grinned. "It would be like feeding the audience little breadcrumbs and then finally revealing the big story at the end. I like that strategy."

Lincoln chuckled. "I started with the announcement from the family doctor, 'Lord Mervin, your wife's child is not yours, the one below stairs looks more like you than this one. This one favors the bookkeeper!'"

Tiana grinned. "You sound very authentic."

"I had tea with Sir Reginald three times this week," Lincoln confessed. "He is a wealth of information, and he makes some beautiful suggestions. Besides, I am a sucker for picking up accents easily."

"If it isn't the favorites." Krista hissed.

Tiana jumped. She hadn't heard Krista's approach.

"Lincoln who is monopolizing Sir Reggie's time and ideas, and Tiana who spends her days and probably nights with James Dalton. They should just declare this competition over with and you two as winners.

Tiana frowned. "Have you finally gone crazy?"

"The two of you are not playing fair." Krista glared at her

and then Lincoln, "It's obvious that you are both sucking up to James and Sir Reggie."

"There are two other judges," Lincoln said. "I see the other writers spending time with them or sucking up as you call it."

"They are not the key judges," Krista grunted and then looked at Tiana. "Have you called your brother yet?"

"I didn't have the time." Tiana shrugged. "I am too busy sucking up to James. By the way, if you want me to do a favor for you, defaming me in public is not going to help your cause."

"I am sorry." Krista tried to look contrite. "I am known to be wrong."

She went back to her seat by the window with Lesley, and the two of them preceded to whisper.

Tiana looked at Lincoln. "I don't like those two together."

Lincoln shrugged. "What's the worst that they can do?"

Tiana's phone rang, and she looked at the call display. It was Elsa.

"I'll be back." She left the library and went outside into the great hall.

"Just checking in," Elsa said. "How is it going?"

"It's going okay," Tiana whispered and then looked around. No one was in earshot. She spoke louder. "I am almost done with the work. It is actually fun."

"And James?" Elsa chuckled, "how is it going with him?"

"Good." Tiana grinned, "very good."

"Have you called Cole and broken up with him yet?"

"No." Tiana sighed, "not looking forward to it. Have you started job hunting yet?"

"Yep. Just put out a few feelers called a few people." Elsa growled. "Apparently, I am blacklisted in the industry. Everybody heard that I was fired by Geo King because I was coming on to him. Can you believe that? Word is, I pursued him and got aggressive when he declared his love for his wife, and then I threatened to kill him and his family if he didn't make love to me."

"Are you serious?" Tiana was genuinely shocked.

"As a judge." Elsa gritted out. "The story is so ludicrous I thought that it would be laughed off, but when a rich, powerful idiot speaks, the rest of the other rich idiots who are hiring, lap it up like it is gospel."

"Have you told Toddy?" Tiana heard a sound toward the front entrance, and she spun around.

It was Brian Morgan. He waved to her and headed in the direction of the library.

She waved back.

"I am not telling Toddy anything," Elsa said tiredly. "He has been hinting that he wants me to do him a favor. I don't want to be beholden to Toddy for this."

"Okay, I get you." Tiana lowered her voice, "before I forget, I should tell you that there is a girl here who looks a lot like the Pryces. Her name is Krista Pryce, James' ex-fiancé. I think she is related to us, Els."

"Oh, really?" Elsa sounded fascinated. "What's her mother's name?"

"Ah," Tiana wracked her brain, "Annessa Baylor, but she is dead. She was a high-class prostitute."

"Toddy doesn't need to pay for sex." Elsa snorted. "He's not the dad. Maybe it is Paul, doesn't he live in Montego Bay at certain times of the year?"

"Maybe." Tiana shrugged. "I am still going to tell Toddy. He'll sort it out."

"You do that," Elsa said, "but don't mention that I need a job. I don't want him interfering."

****

Tiana tried to call Toddy, but his phone rang without an answer. She eventually left him a voice message, Toddy it's Tiana, I am in St. Ann at the Morgan Great House for a job interview, and I met a girl named Krista Pryce, she said her mother's name was Annessa Baylor. If you know anything about this call me back. By the way, she looks like us, same eyes, she looks like a young Caroline.

She hung up the phone and spun around to head to the library.

Brian met her halfway across the hall. "Tiana, we meet again. I was searching for James or my father. They are not answering their phones. Have they left the premises?"

Tiana smiled. "I think James is gone for the day. I haven't seen Sir Reggie."

Brian smiled. "Have you knocked them off their feet yet?"

"Not yet." Tiana smiled, "deadline is tomorrow. I will hear what my fate is on Sunday."

"What are you doing this weekend?" Brian winked at her. "I know a place quite close to here where they serve the best, and I mean the best food."

Tiana laughed. "I am going home. I have a choir engagement at church this weekend in the morning, and then I have a group song at a wedding in the evening, it will be a packed day."

"You sing?" Brian raised an eyebrow. "I don't believe it."

"Why not?" Tiana frowned. "I don't look like I sing?"

"Nah," Brian grinned, "I once knew a girl, she resembled you a bit, she joined a church choir just so that she could drown out her voice in the group. If you heard her doing a solo your ears would bleed."

"I have no reason to prove that I can sing." Tiana folded her arms. "Nice try though, Brian Morgan."

"What's the song that are you singing for the wedding?"

Brian asked. "Give me a verse."

Tiana chuckled. "You are persistent."

"Humor me, Tiana, walk me to the car. No one will hear you."

"Okay since you begged," Tiana said. "I could use the break."

Brian headed down the great house steps and then turned back to her. "Start."

"The bride requested that we sing, This Year's Love, David Gray, they have been off and on for a while. She thought it would be appropriate."

"Okay." Brian spread his arms. "Do it."

This year's love had better last, Heaven knows it's high time…Tiana imagined she was hearing the haunting piano notes.

When she was finished. Brian stared at her, stunned. "Tiana, you can sing."

"Told you." Tiana grinned, "now can I go back to writing?"

"Wait," Brian grinned, "do you know, I can sing too. He started singing, Just the Way You Are, by Bruno Mars. Oh, her eyes, her eyes make the stars look like they're not shinin', Her hair, her hair falls perfectly without her trying…"

He sounded good.

Tiana laughed. "I thought you were gay!"

"Shh, not so loud." Brian looked around him. "I was bi-curious in college. My curiosity was well and truly satisfied then. I am on the straight and narrow now. James must really like you, he never pulls out the Brian is gay card, unless he is feeling threatened by me."

Tiana smiled. "I really must go, Brian."

"Me too." Brian looked at his watch. "I am going to make another effort to find my father. Have a great weekend."

She nodded and went back inside; the library was empty.

Lincoln, Lesley, and Krista and her computer were no longer there.

Tiana’s first impulse was to panic but instead she went searching. Maybe Lincoln had put away her laptop. Ten minutes later she still couldn't find it. She went out into the great house area and looked around. The place was eerily empty.

Chapter Seventeen

Tiana didn't know how long she sat on the top steps of the great house, stewing in her mind. It was probably an hour later that James, Traci, and Sir Reggie showed up.

"Tiana, what's wrong?" James asked, urgently. He must have taken one look at her devastated face and knew something was off.

"Somebody is trying to sabotage me!" Tiana said weak tears were gathering at the side of her eyes.

"My laptop is missing! With my work on it, this is it the end of the road. There is just one day left for the deadline. I searched through the whole place and can't find it."

By the time she finished talking, she was hyperventilating.

James and Sir Reggie looked concerned but not alarmed.

"Someone must have put it up for you," James offered.

"Or hid it to knock you out of the competition," Sir Reggie said. "Who was in the room when you were last there?"

"Lincoln, Krista, and Lesley," Tiana said panic taking over.

"Maybe Lincoln took it up for you," Sir Reggie offered. "He is a good chap. I like the way his mind works."

"I'll call them." Traci offered, heading into the house.

James nodded. "You'll get your machine back in no time."

Tiana inhaled raggedly. "This is not shaping up to be the best day for me at all. There is also a huge chunk of Anastacia's diary missing from the jump drive I got."

"Whatever do you mean?" Sir Reggie asked. "Come, have a late lunch with us and tell us about this."

Tiana inhaled raggedly. "Okay. I was hoping to fine-tune a couple of things and finish up today."

"You can tell us about your plot angle as well," Sir Reggie said, "I am dying to hear the ideas of everyone. So far, I have only heard from about half the writers. It's going to be hard to choose."

Tiana nodded. She couldn't refuse, even though she didn't know if she could eat a bite.

****

Lunch was not as anxiety ridden as Tiana thought it would be. Sir Reggie was entertaining, She told them about the missing pages in the electronic diary. He waved it off.

Traci will sort that out.

He proceeded to ask her about her family. She figured it was on behalf of Krista that his curiosity was stirred. She told him what she knew. He confessed that he donated to some charity of Toddy's and that they knew each other briefly.

He was in the middle of one of his entertaining tales when Traci appeared on the patio.

"Sorry to interrupt, but neither Lesley, Krista nor Lincoln has seen your laptop." Traci shook her head. "Sorry, Tiana."

Tiana subsided in her chair. "Are you sure?"

"I am sure that's what they said." Traci looked at her sorrowfully, "Lincoln said he left Krista and Lesley in the library. He thought you were coming back shortly. He heard you singing on the steps with Brian."

Tiana nodded. "Yes, I was trying to demonstrate that I could sing, then he sang too. And I got a bit carried away."

James snorted.

Tiana looked at him and grinned. "Brian has a lovely voice."

"Krista said she left for home and Lesley said she went walking. She didn't take note whether your laptop was there or not."

"But it can't just walk away." Tiana insisted. "Someone took it. I only stepped away for about twenty minutes. One of them is trying to sabotage me. I vote Krista, she hates me."

"I don't think we should jump to conclusions," Sir Reggie said gently. "However, it might very well be Krista. We will get to the bottom of this, don't worry."

"And you can use my laptop in the interim," James offered. "If you want to continue writing today."

"I had three days' worth of work on there." Tiana ran her fingers through her hair. "How on earth am I going to recreate that in twenty-four hours?"

"What was your idea?" Sir Reggie asked unperturbed.

He could afford to be calm about the whole thing, he wasn't in the competition. It wasn't his work that was missing.

Tiana inhaled and then looked at James and Traci. "Maybe I shouldn't tell you guys…"

Traci pulled a chair and sat down. "You should. I am all ears."

"Well, I…" Tiana drummed her fingers on the table, "I thought of telling the story from the butler's perspective, starting with meeting Merv Morgan at the dock in Haiti…I also thought of naming the show the Butlers Diary…"

She went on and on, nobody stopped her.

When she finished speaking. Sir Reggie was nodding. "I think that is brilliant. I like it, a new plantation, a new beginning, a good introduction to the key players with a commentator. I am not sure about the title, the Butlers Diaries but the more I think of it, the more it is growing on me."

"I was thinking of showing Anastacia's side of the story too. When she is forced to marry the new neighbor. That's why I was in the library, to read the diaries."

"I like it too," Traci said, "the narrator's voice puts a nice spin on it, like Desperate Housewives they had a narrator, it worked."

"Yes!" Tiana nodded.

"I'll take a look at the jump drive." Traci got up. "I have so many copies, something must have happened with that one."

Tiana turned to James. "So what do you think?"

"I'll reserve my judgment until I see what you have," James smiled at her. "I like the name The Butlers Diary. I love it actually. As I said, you can use my laptop. In the meantime, Sir Reggie will make sure that you get back yours. There are cameras in the library. The security team will check the feeds, and we'll see who the culprit is."

"And you knew all of this while I sat here agonizing over it," Tiana said, "no wonder you were taking this so well."

James shook his head. "We all wanted to hear what you were working on and calm you down a bit. It sounds promising."

"And whoever hid your laptop will be asked to leave immediately," Sir Reggie said. "It was not a sporting thing to do, it was petty and mean."

Tiana nodded. "Thank you."

****

"I hope it's Krista," Tiana said when they were in the library again. James brought his laptop and sat across from her.

"I know enough about her to know that she is not vindictive like that." James shrugged, "However, people can change and surprise you."

"But if it's not her that would leave Lesley and Lincoln. I like them both. Well, Lincoln more than Lesley. Lesley is a dark horse; I don't know why she would take my laptop. I shared the information that I got about the butler with her first. Of course, she begged me not to tell anyone. Krista, on the other hand, I can see her doing this to confuse me. I loathe that girl."

"We'll just have to wait and see," James said. "I am never quick to jump to conclusions about people, you shouldn't be either. Krista could be your sister or niece or cousin or something. You may regret saying you loathe her."

"It would actually be normal if we disliked each other," Tiana muttered. "The Pryce side of my family is like that. She'd fit right in."

"Krista had a tough life," James said. "I think that is why we bonded when we were younger. She had never met her mother or father; her aunt Beatrice was childless and didn't want any children, and my parents were in transit in my life. I hardly saw my mother when I was younger and my father only once or twice a year."

"All three of us have that in common then… no parents, except I am the only real orphan in all of this," Tiana mused, "no sympathy from me for you two."

"Touché." James chuckled. "However, I believe that

knowing that your parents are alive but that they are not giving you attention is a whole other ball game. It does something to the psyche."

"You are right." Tiana looked at him. "What did it do to your psyche?"

"It made me more tolerant, more patient to other people's shortcomings. It made me grateful for the people I have in my life."

"So a positive effect then?" Tiana nodded, "got it."

"And how did it affect your psyche?" James asked, "not having parents?"

"I have abandonment issues," Tiana said truthfully. "I am engaged to a man because I love his family. I want what they have. I am messed up and shouldn't even be bringing this up. You have a therapeutic effect on me. Have you thought about doing psychology?"

James leaned his head to one side. "You were honest with yourself, and then you deflect, mmm…"

"Mmm, nothing. I have to work." Tiana opened the laptop. There was a music screen on display. I am Ready For Love, India Arie.

Tiana looked up at him wide-eyed. "This is on your playlist?"

James nodded. "I like the song."

"Well, then…" Tiana was shocked, "You realize that this has been my anthem for years? When I was in your class, especially. I made a checklist with this and compared you to it."

"And how did I do?" James asked. "I love music, art, respect the spirit world, and think with my heart."

"So does Cole," Tiana sighed. "I should get on with this."

James nodded. "Let me leave you to it."

Tiana looked at him, gratefully. "Thank you for your laptop

and the therapy. You are a nice person, James. I mean it. I never really thought of you as nice before. I was always in awe of your looks, which is a strike against me. I objectified you, and I was shallow."

James smiled, his green eyes sparkling. "Thank you for that Tiana, now that statement gives me hope that we have a genuine friendship going. See you later."

Tiana blushed and looked back at the laptop. When she looked up again, he was gone.

****

James didn't want to admit it to anyone, but he was steaming mad. Why would anyone want to take Tiana's laptop? He had projected calm around her, but he was very troubled about it.

He entered the bookkeeper's residence and headed straight for the back where the security station was. Sir Reggie had put up an intricate security system on the property years ago that was unobtrusive to guests. They had no idea that the place was more guarded than Fort Knox or that his uncle had twenty-four hours security on the property.

"Who did it?" He asked before he reached into the room fully.

Sir Reggie and his security officer looked up from the video they were poring over.

"Lesley." Sir Reggie straightened up. "Krista got up to take a call. Lesley took up the laptop and slipped it into her bag, after rifling through Tiana's notes."

James exhaled raggedly. "I am happy it wasn't Krista."

"Me too," Sir Reggie said. "Well then, where is Lesley?"

The security officer looked up. "She is heading for the cottage area."

"Good." James nodded, "I'll go retrieve the laptop and

then ask her to leave."

"Oh, we are coming with you, Sir." The security officer said, "in case there is trouble and to make sure she leaves the great house property."

James nodded. "Very well."

****

Lesley didn't put up much of a fight. She looked at the security and then at James and nodded in resignation. "You are here for the laptop."

"Yes," James said, "and we are asking you to leave. This is not in the spirit of the competition."

"The competition?" Lesley widened her eyes, "but why? It was just a prank. Tiana was moving so fast. I thought I would slow her down a bit."

"It was cruel," James said, "when would you have given her back her laptop?"

"Tomorrow morning!" Lesley said, "I swear. She would then have to scramble to get stuff done. I didn't mean any harm, I swear."

She went to her room and came back out with the laptop. "I couldn't even get into the dratted thing it is password protected."

"So you tried to access her work?" James asked.

"Yes," Lesley nodded, "I wanted to see how far she was. I didn't mean anything by this."

James went to the door. "You have an hour to leave. The security officer will escort you off the premises."

Krista said she was your favorite, Lesley hissed when he was at the door. "She said you were in love with Tiana from high school. You are not morally superior to me, James Dalton!"

James continued out of the door without looking back. He didn't have an appropriate truthful comeback.

Chapter Eighteen

Tiana submitted her manuscript to Traci at the nick of time on Friday evening.

"You made it on time." Traci grinned at her. "I hope you make the cut."

"Me too," Tiana said with a sigh. "If I do, I guess I will see you on Monday. If not, it was nice meeting you."

Traci smiled. "Likewise Tiana, enjoy your weekend."

Tiana nodded. She had already packed up all her stuff and put them in her car. James was leaning on it when she reached outside, sunglasses perched on his curls.

"You had quite a week, didn't you?" He folded his arms.

"Quite a week." Tiana sighed. "And I am going to have quite a weekend."

"Plans with Cole?" James asked, casually.

"Nope. Not really." Tiana grimaced. "I have church and a wedding."

"Break it off with him," James said. "Make a clean cut."

Tiana looked at him speechless. “Why should I?”

“Because you didn’t accomplish your goal, here. You didn’t burn me out of your system. I am still in your head.”

“Well, I…” Tiana looked at him searchingly. “Maybe I will never burn you out of my system. Maybe I am just destined to be a James Dalton groupie, but that won’t do me any good. Maybe we'll never get together until sixty-odd years from now.”

“I am sure we will see each other in the intervening years,” James touched her on the cheek briefly, “before you lose your teeth, and I lose my sight.”

“I’ll miss our morning walks," Tiana said huskily.

“Me too.” James stepped back, “Bye, Tiana.”

“Bye, James.” Tiana inhaled roughly.

She got in the car, watched him in the rearview until he was no longer there, and wondered why she felt so bereft. It had been a week, one week, and yet she felt as if she had never missed anyone this much in her life.

She listened to music all the way into Kingston, trying not to think. Her first stop was at Yara's apartment.

Yara took her time to get to the door when she called her on the phone to open up. She glared at Tiana. “You didn’t call me all of this week. I called you and left messages. I should have made you wait a little longer.”

“So standing out here was punishment?” Tiana chuckled. “I am sorry about this week. I just didn’t want to delve too much in my normal life. I was glad for the break to be honest.”

She walked into Yara’s place and closed the door behind her. Yara was still in her work clothes. “You just got in?”

“Yes.” Yara snarled. “I just got in. I had to call Elsa to ask her if she spoke to you and she said yes. That’s when I knew you were okay.”

"I sent you a text," Tiana said weakly.

"A text!" Yara glared at her. "You and I do not have a text kind of relationship. So you met up with James Dalton and all of a sudden, I am in the back seat…my brother is in the back seat. Everything else in your normal life is in the back seat?"

"I guess you and James reconnected over the past week and now you are going to marry him tomorrow."

Tiana grinned and sat in one of Yara's overstuffed settees. Her patio doors were opened, and she could look outside at the city lights. "I've always liked the view from your apartment."

"You are changing the subject." Yara stood in front of her. "What gives, Tiana? How was your five days away?"

"Enlightening." Tiana said, "and tiring and weirdly exhilarating."

"Yes, James Dalton always gave you the thrills," Yara said disparagingly.

"I am not talking about James. I mean writing a script in five days. It was exhilarating."

"Oh." Yara sat across from her. "And did you sort out your feelings for James?"

"Yes, while driving down I realized that I love him. I always did, maybe I always will. I somehow felt the real thing when I was a teenager. It wasn't a fluke. It wasn't madness. I just didn't know how to handle it then. I was immature and went overboard, but I know what I am doing now. I want to get to know him better, we agreed to be friends."

"Friends!" Yara snorted. "You and I are friends. You don't need any other friend. You need my brother. My mom and I have already picked the wedding colors."

"You can't guilt me into this," Tiana said appalled. "You told me to sort out my feelings for James."

"I thought there wouldn't be any feelings!" Yara stood up. "Who keeps up feelings for somebody they haven't seen in six years. Who still has a thing for someone six years later? Normal people move on."

"And why is James Dalton still single? What's wrong with the women in his circle? What's wrong with him?"

Tiana chuckled. "I am going home. I have to rest up for church."

"We have a family dinner on Sunday," Yara said. "My mom thought it would be nice to have an engagement party with just us and the extended family."

"I can't do it." Tiana shook her head. "I can't make it."

"You can and you will," Yara said threateningly. "Tiana, my brother is a catch. Do you know how many women would like to be in your shoes right now? You are crazy for throwing away a two-year relationship for no promises, no stability, no nothing, just friendship with a guy who probably has a long list of broken hearts in his wake. You'll just be a friend with benefits."

"You said you liked it when I threw caution to the wind," Tiana said stubbornly. "This is me throwing caution to the wind."

"Maybe a week wasn't enough for you to fully appreciate how hopeless James Dalton is," Yara said. "Then again if you don't get through to the next round, he probably won't go out of his way to see you, and you'll have to face facts. The man just isn't interested in you."

"You said that a bit too hopefully," Tiana accused her friend.

"Of course, I want what's best for you," Yara said in exasperation. "Just come to the stupid engagement party, my mother has been slaving over it, she already invited the whole clan. I mean everybody is excited about this, both sets of grandparents, the uncles, and aunties. Something is definitely wrong with you, my friend."

Tiana sighed. "No, something is wrong with you. My happiness does not factor into this for you, just your brother's, but I guess blood is thicker than water."

"Don't say that." Yara softened her tone. "I know you'll be happy with my brother. I just don't think you know it yet."

"I have to go." Tiana murmured feeling pressured. "I need to sleep. I'll be late for church tomorrow." She headed for the door.

"Wait," Yara said. "I thought you'd like to know I have been investigating James Dalton."

"And?" Tiana turned to her. "What skeletons did you find?"

"None." Yara frowned. "Zilch. The man is clean as a whistle, which could be a bad thing."

Tiana chuckled. "Why?"

"Nobody is perfect," Yara warned. "He could be very good at hiding things."

"Or he doesn't have anything to hide." Tiana let herself out.

****

The engagement party was a Carr family event, no friends just family, which meant that there were more than sixty of them in the spacious backyard of the Carr mansion.

"To the future mother of my grandchildren." Naomi Carr raised her glass to Tiana. "May she live long and prosper."

Tiana raised her glass back, wondering fretfully if anybody could see the hunted expression on her face.

"I would like to propose a toast too." Vincent Carr raised his glass. "Tiana, beautiful Tiana, we appreciate you and look forward to you joining our family. We are not a perfect bunch and marriage is hard work, ask anyone of the old-timers here, but we say, love and family support is a good foundation, we will always be here for you both."

"Here here." Glasses were knocked, champagne downed, people cheered. Everybody had marital advice.

"I think we should set the wedding date for July," Cole whispered in her ear.

"You mean July next year?" Tiana asked.

"No, July next month." Cole looked at her possessively. "We've been together for more than two years. Why wait longer?"

"But I have plans." Tiana swallowed. She was staring in Cole's face in a panic. "If I get shortlisted, I'll be spending July and August in St. Ann."

"Scrap those plans," Cole said nonchalantly. "You don't have to do this writing thing, if you don't want to. Surely we are more important than a silly competition."

Tiana opened her mouth to retort, but she was swept up in a hug from one of Cole's aunties. Her name was Paula, and she was the widow of two very wealthy men.

"Listen," Paula pinched her cheek, "if you marry my nephew, I am going to leave half of my fortune to you."

"You don't have to bribe her to marry me." Cole chuckled. "Tiana loves me."

"Ah, you sweet girl." Paula hugged Tiana to her ample bosom again. "Promise you will stay with him for at least five years and have at least one child, and I'll really give you half my fortune. I am worth a lot, you know. His parents may be wealthy, but it's a drop in the bucket compared to what I own. I know you are in it for the money, this would be added incentive. You are such a pretty girl too."

Tiana widened her eyes in consternation. "Excuse me?"

"She's drunk," Cole said good-naturedly. "Aunt Paula,

leave Tiana alone."

"I am not drunk," Paula whispered in Tiana's ear, "but with marriage the way it is in today's society and Cole… did he tell you?"

"Tell me what?" Tiana whispered back.

"That he is a sweet, sweet boy," Paula chuckled, "very sweet boy, our Cole."

"I know he is sweet," Tiana said. "You love him a lot, don't you, Paula?"

"Like he was my own," Paula blinked back tears, "but I know your marriage to him won't last."

"Aunt P, stop." Cole walked over. "What are you telling Tiana?"

"These sort of marriages never do." Paula looked back at Tiana as Cole lead her away. "It's best to follow your heart and not the money."

Tiana didn't know if she was to feel warned or insulted. When Cole took the microphone and announced that they would be having a wedding in July, she didn't know if she should be fuming or laughing.

She didn't feel much of anything. All of this was happening as if it were to someone else. She didn't even protest when Cole dropped her home. They had ridden silently. She was too tired for conversation, and he seemed to be in deep thought.

"Don't let my aunt get to you, she was tipsy," Cole said, looking at her warily.

"It's not just her, it's also the way you announced that we are getting married in July." Tiana pulled her seatbelt. "I am not getting married in July. I really want to be a part of the writing team, and I am going to see this through."

"Fine. Cole mumbled, "but Tiana, I am not going to be one of those guys that stay engaged for ten or more years waiting for you to make up your mind."

Tiana looked at him. "This is clearly not working, Cole."

"Don't say anything." Cole put a finger on her lips.

"If I get a call tonight I'll be away for the week." Tiana moved away from him. "I'll see you this weekend."

He didn't say anything. He watched as she went into the house and then drove away.

Chapter Nineteen

"So you are getting married in a month," Giselle asked over the phone, "In the summer, while I am in Switzerland?"

"For the umpteenth time, No! Cole announced that we were getting married in July. I had no say in his autocratic date setting. I am not even going to let it bother me. All I am doing now is waiting for the confirmation from JD Productions to see if I am accepted in their top six. And that is why I am up so late. I am having some of Elsa's Halo Top ice cream. You know she is gone low carb now. She is even making her own bread and giving me lectures about sugar."

Giselle laughed. "Where is she?"

"She left a note saying that she is gone sailing with the crew. One of her friends has a boat."

"Oh," Giselle snorted. "Why is it so easy for that girl to make friends?"

"I have no clue," Tiana murmured. "She makes no effort to be anybody else but her true authentic self. Take her or leave her. People seem to like that. I have another call. We'll talk soon."

She hung up and answered the other call. It was security announcing that Toddy was at the gate.

It didn't take long before the doorbell rang.

She opened the door and grinned at her brother. "Hey you, I called you last week, and you didn't answer."

"Did you look through the peephole before you opened the door?" Toddy asked sternly.

"Yes." Tiana smiled.

"I am sorry about not calling back. I was going to call today but thought about seeing you in person instead. I was intrigued by your message. "

"Oh, the stuff about Krista."

Toddy headed to the kitchen. "What kind of a Sunday supper is that? Come to my place. Myrna cooked roast fish with roast vegetables. I am sure she has more."

Tiana looked at her ice-cream and licked her lips. She had hardly eaten at the engagement party. Myrna's food would be ten times better.

"I can't, I am expecting a call from JD Productions. If I am shortlisted, I'll have to pack and then head to St. Ann tomorrow morning. I want to be early. I was late the last time."

"That's lovely." Toddy looked at her proudly. "So am I going to see your name on the screen? You, Tiana Pryce, will write an actual television series."

"Yes." Tiana nodded. "I'll be a part of the staff."

"I am so proud of you." Toddy chuckled.

"Don't be, not yet." Tiana sat down and dipped her spoon into the ice cream container. "It's a competition. I may not get in."

"You'll get in," Toddy sat beside her and drummed his

fingers on the island. "How is life? The Cole guy? You said you are now officially engaged?"

"Yes," Tiana nodded, "but I am not sure about this, Toddy."

"Good. I don't like the guy." Toddy sighed. "There is something about him that makes me uneasy."

"You told me you thought he was perfect." Tiana accused.

"Because of his parents," Toddy shrugged. "He is from a good family."

"But you just don't like him personally?" Tiana raised her brow.

"I don't, but it shouldn't matter if I do or don't since you are the one who is going to marry him," Toddy said.

"His aunt Paula said our marriage won't last." Tiana mused. "She offered me money to stay with him for at least five years."

"That's a bad sign." Toddy pretended to shudder. "Very bad sign."

"I know," Tiana murmured. "It was odd the way she did it though. I don't know…maybe she was drunk or bordering on senile as Cole said."

"My first wife's father did that to me, offered me money to stay with his daughter. Nobody in their family had ever divorced, and he wanted to keep the status quo, but he knew his little darling was not on the up and up."

"Obviously you didn't take it " Tiana chuckled.

"Oh, I did." Toddy nodded, "but she was unfaithful to me so many times I reached breaking point. When we finally called it quits her father didn't oppose the divorce. He and I are still on good terms."

"She was unfaithful?" Tiana widened her eyes, "and not you?"

"Not me," Toddy said sadly. "Those days I were different. I thought women didn't get as down and dirty as men. I thought all women were like my saintly mother, boy was I wrong."

"So it's her fault why you are like this?"

"More or less." Toddy shrugged. "She changed my mind about women for sure. Before I forget, I found out about Krista Pryce for you."

"Yes," Tiana swallowed and then wiped her lips. "Is she your love child? Did you recognize the mother's name?"

Toddy grinned. When he did Tiana could see why women of all ages found him so charming.

"I don't know if she is my love child. I don't recognize the mother's name. I do know that Caroline's nickname was Krista. Caroline Krista Pryce. I haven't heard the name Krista in years. It was enough for me to call her about it, and after several investigations, we have pieced together an incredible story."

"What story?" Tiana asked, her eyes wide.

"After several phone calls and shaking of family trees the story goes like this." Toddy smirked. "You know Caroline had a son, Arnold? He is her only child."

"I never met him, she never mentioned him," Tiana shook her head, "and I stayed with her for two whole weeks one Christmas, and she never mentioned having a child."

"They haven't spoken to each other for years. Arnold is living in Germany with his father's family." Toddy shrugged. "Caroline was not the warmest parent in the world, but she had lofty ideals for her son, but he couldn't live up to them, so they are not on speaking terms."

"I see." Tiana nodded. "So what does that have to do with Krista?"

"Well, Arnold came to Jamaica every year for spring break and stayed at Paul's place in Montego Bay. He partied like it was going out of style, took various women to the place, and had a good time.

"Paul said he vividly remembered a woman showing up at the house to tell him that she was pregnant. He had never seen her in his life, but the woman insisted that the house was where she had several trysts with a younger guy also named Paul Pryce.

"Paul put two and two together and found out that Arnold was using his name with his various women. He called Arnold told him about the lady who claimed to be pregnant. Arnold didn't remember her and ignored the situation, and that is the story."

"So why did Krista's mother name the child Krista?" Tiana asked.

"Don't know." Toddy shook his head. "It could be a coincidence, or maybe Arnold told her that he hates the name Krista, and she named the child in revenge. Who knows?"

"Are you sure it isn't Paul, who is the father?" Tiana frowned.

"Nope." Toddy shook his head, "Paul is firing blanks, had a bad case of mumps when he was younger. His two children are adopted."

"Oh." Tiana opened her mouth. "I didn't know that. So, in other words, Krista's father doesn't want to know about her."

"Yep." Toddy nodded. "Caroline said she would like to meet her though which is a good thing. Caroline has mellowed through the years. She said she would call you for the girl's number."

"She looks like her," Tiana grimaced, "exactly like her."

"Send Caroline a picture," Toddy said. "She'll like the fact that she has a grandchild that looks like her and one that is accessible. I am sure that there is some monetary benefit in there for this Krista. If she plays her cards right, she might just be the recipient of her grandmother's fortune. Caroline will not leave it to Arnold."

Tiana nodded. "Okay, I'll do that. What is Arnold's last name? Maybe Krista would want to do some research on her own."

"Wagner." Toddy drummed his fingers on the table. "His father was a lawyer like Caroline. They divorced before the child was a year old, Caroline got custody."

"I see." Tiana shrugged. "Maybe one day Krista will meet Arnold and find closure. This family is truly messed up."

"Only some of us." Toddy sighed. "I think you Gis and Elsa are okay."

"Thanks, Toddy." Tiana grinned, "but I am not so sure about me right now."

****

The phone call came in almost at midnight. Tiana was having a difficult time sleeping anyway.

"Hello," Traci sounded chirpy, "I am pleased to inform you that you are on for the next round."

"Really?" Tiana squeaked.

"Oh, yes," Traci said. "The final six was an easy pick, and your script was one of two that was very strong. When you come by tomorrow, we will divide you into two groups of three. The group with the best episode based on the pilot wins. See you then."

After Traci hung up, Tiana jumped out of bed and started packing. Elsa wandered into her room, sleepily and curled up on the bed.

"So, you are shortlisted."

"Yes, ma'am," Tiana said excitedly. "Yes, I am."

"Congrats, love." Elsa yawned. "I'll be rooting for you."

"Thanks." Tiana grinned.

"Did Krista get in?" Elsa murmured sleepily.

"I don't know." Tiana made a face.

"Well, you'll have to tell her about Caroline and Arnold and all of that jazz."

"Yup." Tiana stood in front of the closet. There was no fancy dressing or even work clothes involved. Just jeans and shirts and walking clothes.

She'd be walking with James in the mornings!

"You are not listening to me, are you?" Elsa muttered.

"Nope." Tiana glanced at her sister. "Don't fall asleep in my bed."

"I don't see why not?" Elsa closed her eyes. "You are my only company. Tell me about Cole."

"There is nothing to tell. I gave you all the details when you got in a couple hours ago." Tiana murmured. "Without my consent he is setting a wedding date for July."

"I wonder what's the rush." Elsa pointed at a green blouse. "Wear that."

Tiana nodded. "It's the same shade as James' eyes."

Elsa got up. "Okay then that's my cue to leave. I don't want you to go on and on about James. Goodnight. Love you."

"Love you too, Els," Tiana said distractedly. "I hope you find a job soon. I hate it when you sound so down."

"Maybe I am going to have to do something else," Elsa muttered. "I caught a fish today. Maybe I could make it work as a fisherman."

Chapter Twenty

There were two disappointments when Tiana drove up to Morgan Great House for the second time. James was not there, he had business to deal with in California, however Krista was there, looking as smug as ever and was a part of the final six.

This second week was going to suck without James, Tiana thought darkly.

"And then there were six," Traci announced when they were gathered in the library. "Congrats to the six of you. Two scripts stood out. We want to see where you will go with both, The Butlers Diary by Tiana Pryce and Morgan's Ardor by Krista Pryce."

Tiana looked over at Krista sharply, whose eyes connected with hers as well. The same expression of shock reflected in her stare.

"Which means that the two scripts will have two leaders," Jose said, "and they will choose from the remaining four who they want to work with. We have the names in a bag, so this will be random selection."

Tiana went first. She was happy to get Lincoln and another writer, Josette.

Krista got Hillary and Linda.

"All girls." Krista grinned. "I like this, we'll crush you three."

Tiana didn't comment. She wasn't so confident. She didn't know how she would get on with Lincoln or Josette. They would have to buy into her vision for the series. She wondered if they would butcher her work.

"So you have a two-hour episode to write for the week. The deadline is Friday midday. This challenge is more about working within a group and producing quality work on time, that's going to be important when you are a part of a writing team.

"This means, your work has to be in by twelve on Friday afternoon, no exceptions.

"A three- room cottage will be available to both groups. You can work around the clock or you can chill. Just remember the deadline is key."

Traci smiled. "Let the games begin. Jose is your only resource at this time. James will be back on Friday. And as usual Sir Reggie says he will be at your service if you need his input."

****

Lincoln and Josette read her work the first day, by day two they worked together to outline the second episode, by day three they were putting it down on paper, the three of them doing their assigned parts.

They had good camaraderie, so they worked seamlessly

together. Josette was a stickler for details and Lincoln had the best suggestions.

"What kind of music did they listen to in the eighteenth century?" Lincoln yelled. He was on the patio. He said he worked better staring at the greenery.

Tiana and Josette were sitting at the dining table.

"Baroque music, Bach, Vivaldi, Telemann." Josette was the one who answered. "Why?"

"Was just thinking about framing the scene." Lincoln responded.

Tiana grinned; Lincoln liked to use the word frame.

They were invited to the great house for dinner on Thursday evening by Sir Reggie. That was the first time Tiana was seeing Krista since Monday.

****

"I liked your title," Krista said grudgingly.

Tiana grinned. "Not bad for an amateur, huh."

"No." Krista frowned. "How is it going with your group, working like a well-oiled machine?"

"Yes," Tiana nodded, "we are almost done. It is easier when you have more than one writer. I thought I wouldn't be able to collaborate, but it was fun."

Krista snorted. "I can't work with the two I chose. They are driving me crazy. First, they took a long time to finish reading the pilot, then they critiqued it and tried to improve upon it. I told them that it was not the task at hand, but do they care? No. Hillary thinks my dialogue is clunky and the other one can't make up her mind about anything. I wish I had your group."

"I thought you were going to crush us." Tiana laughed. "I am sorry, but you can't get my team, we are almost done."

"Are you serious?" Krista moaned. "Almost done. If I could get the two critics that I am saddled with to get their heads in the game, I could have been saying that now. Instead, I am thinking of downing coffee and doing an all-nighter tonight."

"Sorry." Tiana shrugged.

"No you are not." Krista snorted. "You are probably happy. You see yourself winning, don't you? But don't count me out yet, I am a survivor."

"I found out who your potential father is." Tiana changed the subject.

"You did?" Krista put down her drink and stared at Tiana in shock. "Well that was quick."

"I told the right person in the family; Toddy talks to everybody and everybody talks to him. He said your name sounded familiar when I told him. Actually, it is our sister Caroline's middle name."

"Caroline is your grandmother; her son Arnold is your father. Of course Caroline wants to verify all of this, so she wants your number and she wants to arrange for you to do a DNA test. She and her son have not talked for years, so I don't know how that part of it will go. As I told you before this is not the best of families."

"Oh," Krista gasped, "this is exciting! I mean really good news! I just wanted to know who I am related to biologically. Now I do."

"I guess that makes you my grandniece." Tiana smirked. "Since your father would be my nephew. I never met him by the way. His name is Arnold Wagner."

"Not Pryce?" Krista frowned.

"It's a long story," Tiana said. "I am going to have to sum it up for you when you have the time."

"I am all ears," Krista said resigned. "This is something I

really want to hear."

****

Tiana went out for a walk Friday morning. It was not as early as her daily walks with James, but it was overcast and quite pleasant outside. She and her group were done. It had been somewhat of a breeze to write the first episode, using the narrators voice made it easy. Last night they finished after Lincoln framed the last scene.

It was an overcast morning, so she decided to walk by the great house, the gardeners were out en masse trimming the edges. They waved to her as she passed by. She waved back.

"Tiana!" She spun around. It was Brian. He was in a track suit and he was panting.

"Hey!" Tiana grinned at him.

"I did the hill run," Brian grunted, "down the village and back in ten minutes. That's a ten-minute mile. I am fit."

"Good for you." Tiana chuckled. "I didn't know you were here."

"I came in last night." Brian panted, "I am staying the weekend. "

"You weren't joking when you said you loved it here," Tiana mused.

"To be honest there is a woman in the village I am interested in." Brian inhaled.

"There is always a woman." Tiana chuckled, "I knew you coming back here on the weekends to you see your parent wasn't the main attraction."

"Guilty as charged." Brian grinned. "My father, as lovely as he is doesn't have the kind of pull like my village girl."

"Village girl, huh?" Tiana smiled. "Somehow, I never pictured you with a village girl."

"Me either," Brian chuckled, "but this girl is the one. I am certain about it. But I have an issue. She is ultra conservative, and I have to tell her about my past."

"Oh," Tiana grimaced. "You mean your bi-curious past?"

"Yes." Brian stopped. "When I told you it didn't faze you, did it?"

"No." Tiana shook her head, "but then again I am not interested in you like that."

"That's what I am afraid of." Brian sighed, "my village girl is going to run the other way when I tell her."

"Just tell her, get it over with, if you are as serious as you say." Tiana shrugged, "it is always good to know."

Brian looked away from her and then back. "That's what I …" He sighed. "I am just going to come right out and tell you this. I've seen you before this, Tiana. I knew about you before I saw you in the parking lot when you just arrived here."

"You did?" Tiana groaned. "Of course, you did James told you about me from my high school days?"

"No, I saw your picture at the gallery in Cole Carr's office. He said you were his girlfriend and that he was planning some elaborate plot to ask you to marry him."

"It is a small world. Cole does business with everyone, and he insists on plastering my paintings everywhere."

"Indeed, it is a small world," Brian nodded. "I went to college with Cole. He was doing law; I was doing business. We were roommates. I told you I experimented in college."

Tiana nodded feeling her skin prickle.

"Cole was the reason I even experimented in the first place. He and I had a couple of intimate moments. None of the hardcore stuff, I found out I wasn't as into it as he was. After the first semester I started seeing girls again. He moved on to a guy."

Tiana gasped. "I don't want to hear anymore. I can't listen to this."

"A couple weeks ago he asked me to go home with him, after a business meeting."

Tiana was staring at Brian in shock.

"I turned him down. I had to explain that what we did in college was just me being a horny kid, but it obviously meant something to him, and he is still into that kind of thing now."

"Wow." Tiana sat down on the church steps. "Just wow."

Brian stopped in front of her.

"I asked him about you, obviously because your paintings and pictures are everywhere. He said you are a different part of his life. I told him that he should come clean with you. He told me he would never do it, you two were going to get married, have kids and live your traditional life, just like what his family expected."

Tiana laughed dryly. "His aunt warned me. She knows."

Brian looked at her puzzled, "What?"

"I am just getting it." Tiana rubbed her neck. "She warned me that the marriage wouldn't last five years. She even said I was probably in it for the money. Implying that I would turn a blind eye to him being gay. His entire family probably knows. That's why they are so eager to get us married!"

"I don't know if they know." Brian stretched his neck. "Cole said that they would die if they knew. It's not something that would cross their minds about him. You are taking it well. I actually thought you would be in a puddle crying."

"I knew that something was not quite right between us." Tiana grimaced, "I had a thing for James in high school and I thought if I couldn't recreate it with Cole, it wouldn't be worth it."

Brian nodded. "Maybe subconsciously your mind was telling you to stay away from Cole"

"Yes," Tiana turned to Brian. "Thank you for telling me about Cole. You didn't have to; we only met a couple of times and you have been more honest with me than the people in my life."

She got up and brushed off her track suit.

"Do you want company walking back?" Brian seemed to sense that she was deep in thought.

"No." Tiana looked at him. "Thank you, Brian. I genuinely mean it."

"I had to let you know, it was on my mind." Brian saluted her. "Take care, Tiana."

He veered off toward the bookkeeper's house and Tiana continued toward the cottage, her mind racing.

Should she tell Yara? Did Yara already know?

The thought was repugnant. If Yara knew and didn't tell her. It would break up their friendship. Tiana scowled. As for Cole, she thought about all their times together. Scene by scene. She really never had a clue. She was always just worried that she wasn't as passionate about him as he was about her.

She had even prayed about her lukewarm response to him.

This was an answer to prayer! When things didn't work out, when there is lack of feeling and genuine affection, there was no need to push it. There had been nothing wrong with her all along.

Something was wrong with Cole. He was using her as his cover.

She was his beard!

"I was a beard," Tiana said it out loud. The thought made her falter. She reached the stone bench under the poui tree and sat down with her head in her hand. "A beard."

"Tiana," James said over her head. "You don't have a beard."

"Huh." She almost gave herself a whiplash when she raised her head to look up at James. "Where'd you come from?"

"I came in late last night. Started my day late, decided to walk this way, hoping to bump into you. Is this what the writing is doing to you? You are wondering if you have a beard?"

Tiana drummed up a smile. "No I was wondering if Cole had me as his beard. You know, a man or woman used as a cover for a gay partner. That's why he paints me so much. That's why he takes such pride in plastering my picture everywhere, look, I have a pretty girlfriend. I am heterosexual isn't it obvious?"

Tears came to Tiana's eye. "If I didn't have you in my past to compare what I felt for Cole, I would probably have married him already and thought that, that was the way it was supposed to be. Lukewarm relationship, pretending to be happy when I was dying inside. I would have married a man on the down low and probably had kids with him."

"Oh Tiana." James sat beside her. He looked stunned as well. "How'd you find out?"

"I just had a talk with Brian. He said he was Cole's college roommate and Cole propositioned him recently. Do you know what that means?"

James looked at her sadly. "Unfortunately yes."

"He is probably seeing other men." Tiana gasped. "He said I was in a different compartment of his life. I guess that is how he justifies it."

"You dodged a bullet." James linked their fingers together. "You will be okay. You will move on from this."

"I don't know why I am shocked," Tiana said. "I was going to break up with him anyway. This just hastens that."

"It's unexpected news about someone you care about, and to make it worse the news didn't come from him." James murmured. "The betrayal will fade eventually."

"We sing on the same choir, everyone will wonder." Tiana looked out at the trees in the distance. "They'll wonder what went wrong, they all think we are a perfect couple and then inevitably they'll blame me. Everybody loves Cole, he is a great guy."

"I don't see why anyone has to take the blame for a private matter," James murmured. "Relationships don't work out all the time. Surely the choir members would know that everything has a season. Wasn't that your song?"

"Yup." Tiana nodded, "a time to embrace and a time to stop from embracing."

"And your season with Cole is ending." James squeezed her hand. "Maybe another season with someone else will begin, someone who wants to honor the till death do us part vow."

Tiana looked at him a question in her gaze.

He looked away, a smile on his lips.

Chapter Twenty- One

Tiana drove home on Friday afternoon, feeling a touch melancholy. They had handed in episode one way before the deadline and everybody couldn't wait to get home, including her. She couldn't wait to shut down the Cole chapter of her life.

This time she hadn't even seen James to tell him goodbye. Maybe that accounted for her melancholy. That and the fact that she was mourning her friendship to Yara, it couldn't be the same after this. In a way, that was even more impactful than breaking up with Cole.

Tiana knew deep down that Yara, the Jamaican Nancy Drew, who dabbled in detective work for a hobby, would have some indication that her brother wasn't straight. But yet she had tried with all her might to push her into marrying Cole.

His aunt Paula was the only one who had the courage to warn her. Tiana deliberated going to the Wiley Complex. It was just after one, Yara would probably be at lunch.

She drove in and parked before Yum Yum.

She called Yara. "Hey, want to do lunch today? I am back."

"Hey," Yara said eagerly. "Yes. Where?"

"I am already at Yum Yum."

Tiana got out of the car. Went to order and sat at their usual spot. It took Yara ten minutes to get there.

"You look troubled," Yara said when she sat down with her food. "What's wrong? Did James Dalton tell you in no uncertain terms that you should leave him alone? Did he call the police, and have you chucked out of the place? No wait, has he started seeing his ex again?"

"None of that." Tiana sighed. "I am sad because, I don't think our friendship will survive this."

"Survive what?" Yara widened her eyes.

"Your betrayal. And it's a betrayal. We promised to always have each other's back."

"Now you are scaring me." Yara pushed away her plate. "Stop speaking in riddles. You are back from St. Ann early and you look sad and you speak of betrayal. What on earth do I have to do with this?"

"Cole is gay," Tiana said and when it came out, she was instantly sorry. Yara sat up in the chair like an electric wire had prodded her.

But she didn't look surprised. Tiana looked at her friend with narrowed eyes. It wasn't surprise that was residing in her eyes but fear. Real fear.

"Yara," she prompted Yara who had suddenly gone mute. "Tell me that you didn't know that your brother loved men and that you were not deliberately pushing him and me together in some misguided attempt to straighten him out."

Yara looked at her guiltily and then around. "Tiana, please this is not the time or the place…"

"Tell me," Tiana rasped, "tell me that you didn't know."

"I didn't know for sure, okay," Yara said weakly. "He loves you. He says it over and over again. He paints you constantly, so I thought that my suspicions were unfounded even though I caught him once, a long time ago kissing Dillon from church."

"Dillon?" Tiana widened her eyes. "Our choir director, married with three children?"

"One and the same." Yara squeezed her eyes shut. "It was a long time ago before he left for college in Canada, I convinced myself that I didn't see right. I was sure I was imagining things. I even prayed about my evil imagination."

"You tried to pray your own sight away. You tried to pray reality away?" Tiana hissed. "I think I have heard everything now."

"Listen T, I was over the moon happy when he came to my birthday party and was fixated on you. How did you know that he was er…"

"Gay?" Tiana raised an eyebrow. "You can't say it can you?"

Yara clenched her fists. "I am not a prude. I know these things happen in every family. I just…I didn't want it to happen in mine. I didn't want it to be my brother. I was in denial. Who can blame me? You'd be the same."

"I don't know that I would push my straight best friend or even an enemy to marry my gay brother." Tiana snorted. "Your aunt Paula said those kind of relationships don't last. She called him a sweet, sweet boy…now I am realizing that she was trying to say that he was full of sugar."

"I…" Yara sighed, "how did you find out?"

"I met someone who was intimate with him in college." Tiana sighed, "he warned me about Cole. He said Cole propositioned him when he went to do business with him a couple of weeks ago."

Yara gasped.

"You know what's weird, I only met this person twice. He had no obligation to me whatsoever. He and I were not friends from kindergarten. He and I did not have lunch every day for years. He just thought he should tell me because he did not want me to get hurt by a guy who obviously does not swing for my team!"

Yara covered her eyes and started groaning. "I am sorry T. I mean it. I am so so so so sorry."

"You should have loved me enough to tell me to stay as far away from your down low brother as possible. You didn't have the luxury of staying out of it, Yara. It is me Tiana. You would have pushed me into the type of relationship where I would only end up getting hurt. That was not right. I feel betrayed by you, more than I feel betrayed by Cole."

Yara looked at her, tears in her eyes. "Tiana please, see this from my point of view. He is my brother. I spent years of my life denying my own eyes. He came back from Canada started his own business got involved in church and started dating women. He gushes about you to the family every chance he gets. I was excited about the whole thing. Your children together would be my nieces and nephews. I was in fantasy land. I dismissed what I saw then and I…"

"I am tired." Tiana picked up her lunch, "I am just going to go home. You might not see me around this weekend."

"Wait!" Yara walked behind her until she reached her car.

She opened the door and looked back at Yara's miserable face dispassionately. "Somebody needs to tell Cole that he is not to seek out some female's life to mess up, especially since he is in this frame of mind. Maybe you should be the one to have that conversation with him."

Yara frowned. "I don't know..."

"Coward," Tiana hissed, "think about it, would you like this to happen to you. The next girl might genuinely love him."

Yara didn't answer. Tiana closed the door and drove off.

****

"Cole called me for the fiftieth time. He said he is coming over shortly." Elsa said over her head. "I told him you were sleeping."

Tiana had placed a pillow over her ears.

"There are dozens of roses from him downstairs, each with a juicy sounding card. Here this one, I want to lay you down in a bed of roses…"

"For tonight he'll be sleeping on a bed of nails," Tiana took the pillow off her head. "How appropriate and he doesn't even know."

"What are you going on about?" Elsa asked confused.

"It's the song, Bed of Roses." Tiana looked at Elsa blearily. "What time is it?"

"It's Sunday, after two in the afternoon." Elsa griped. "Did you sleep when you were in St. Ann? You have been at it all weekend."

"Not really." Tiana got out of bed and headed for the bathroom. "It was high pressure; I went to bed late and woke up early."

"I should disappear while Cole is over here, Elsa said. "I don't want to be caught in the middle of an argument."

"Why would you assume we are going to argue?" Tiana shouted from the bathroom.

"Because downstairs is filled with flowers." Elsa came to the bathroom door. "That many flowers means the man is guilty."

"He is guilty of subterfuge," Tiana brushed her teeth and then hopped in the shower, "and frankly so am I. I am going to put us both out of our misery today and then I am going to the gym. Want to come?"

"No." Elsa shook her head. "I am going over to the Wiley Complex. Shawn wants me to install braids in her hair. I am out of a job; I may as well do some hairdressing."

Tiana laughed. "Do you even know how to install braids?"

"I watched a YouTube tutorial." Elsa grinned, "I think I got it."

****

Tiana was downstairs fixing a sandwich when the doorbell rang. The security personnel would have called if it were Cole. She looked through the peephole and saw that it was indeed Cole. He had insinuated that he was going to buy a townhouse in the complex, she dearly hoped he hadn't.

She opened the door. "Hey."

"Hey." Cole grinned at her. "Why am I in the doghouse. You are not answering your phone, you didn't show up for church."

Tiana stepped away from the door. "Come on in."

He reached over to kiss her, and she backed away.

"What's this?" Cole frowned. "Why are you acting weird?"

"Wait a sec." Tiana ran upstairs and got the ring. She had left it in the ring box on her dresser. "I think this is yours." She handed Cole the ring.

"What's going on, Tiana?" Cole frowned.

"I love somebody else." Tiana sighed. "That's the main reason why I am doing this. I always had a thing for him, and I just don't feel the same way about you. I also found out that you aren't straight."

Cole stilled his eyes wide. “Say what?”

“Which part do you want me to repeat?” Tiana asked.

“Who are you in love with?” Cole growled.

“I think I want to address the gay part, first,” Tiana said calmly.

“Whoever you are listening to, is a liar. I am upset that you would even listen to such a thing.”

There wasn’t as much conviction in his voice when he said that. Tiana sighed.

“You should tell your parents, have an honest conversation with them. That’s if they don’t know already. I think they know, your aunt Paula certainly does.”

“I am not gay.” Cole gritted out.

“Bi, gay, polyamorous, on the down low, I don’t know what you are, but we are not getting married.” Tiana looked him dead in the eye. “It’s over. Done.”

“I really love you, Tiana,” Cole inhaled raggedly. “I do slip sometimes. I have a certain…”

Tiana shook her head. “I don’t want to hear it. You don’t owe me any explanations. This is between you and God. I don’t even want to think about it.”

“Are you going to tell anyone?” Cole asked weakly.

“You mean like make a general announcement at church?” Tiana raised an eyebrow. “No, what do you take me for? I’ll tell your new girlfriend or fiancé though. So make sure you tell her first.”

Cole sighed.

“I would have wanted somebody to tell me.” Tiana glared at him. “You and your family are despicable. Your mother knows, doesn’t she?”

Cole nodded. “But my dad doesn’t.”

“I have never seen a future mother-in-law so warm and welcoming. I should have known something was up. They were too happy to embrace me into their fold."

She walked to the door and opened it. "You better say only nice things about me and our breakup or I'll have to be brutally honest to anyone who will listen."

Cole walked through the door and she closed it with a click.

She felt like a burden had been lifted from her chest. Her next stop would have been to call Yara but Yara was off limits for now. It gave her a jolt, but she didn't know if their friendship could ever recover.

She felt a longing to talk to James so badly, but he was probably still judging her work. Wouldn't it be unseemly to call now?

She actually dialed his number and was about to hang-up when he answered on the first ring.

"Hey," she cleared her throat. "I don't know why I called."

"It might be the reason why I was going to call," James said gently. "I missed you this weekend. How did it go with Cole?"

"It's over." Tiana mused.

"So, you are single, I am single and there is not a nursing home in sight." James chuckled. "I think we can preempt the romance by sixty years. Maybe even share the same children together and memories and what not."

Tiana stilled, "James…"

"Of course we are going to take it nice and slow this summer, all of July and August will be ours while we are working closely together, maybe then…"

"My group won?" Tiana whispered.

"Yes." James chuckled. "Congrats, I am sure Traci will call you later. Krista's group had difficulty putting together a cohesive first episode. It was no contest really. You, Lincoln and Josette did a good job as a team. I'm look forward to working with you all this summer."

Epilogue

The end of August

It was a wrap. Eight weeks of writing and building friendships.

James was walking her home to her cottage. He did that every evening without fail. It was drizzling, but Tiana didn't mind. She was in her tracksuit and didn't have on makeup. She hadn't bothered with that since the beginning of the grueling hours they just went through. It had been quite a day.

"So Tiana," James held her hand, "how attached are you to over the top proposals?"

"I er." Tiana stopped, shock making her rigid. They had not talked about the future or what they were going to do next. They hadn't even kissed since that first kiss. James had stayed true to his word and treated her like a friend.

"I am not attached to them." She suddenly felt cold. Her

lips were trembling.

"Good," James murmured, pulling her closer. "I don't have a choir; I just seem to have fallen in love with you. I don't want to lose you when you leave tomorrow. So I humbly want to ask, will you marry me? Be my friend, bride and lover forever."

"Yes!" Tiana managed. "Now this feels right."

"The right Pryce at the right time, I will cherish you forever," James vowed, before he sealed his promise with a kiss.

The End

Here is an excerpt from Yours For A Pryce
(Pryce Sisters Book 3)

"So Tiana is engaged and just finished writing a miniseries, Giselle finished the Diamond League at the top of her event and uninjured." Sharla looked at Elsa with a smile, "and you are bored and unemployed."

"That's about right." Elsa glared at her aunt. "Thanks for the recap. Welcome to the first episode of the Lousiest Pryce Triplet."

Sharla laughed. "Even in your doldrums, you manage to add some creativity and humor to the conversation."

"This is no laughing matter, Aunt Sharla," Elsa groaned. "I am the only of my sisters that is unlucky in love, unlucky in employment and just plain unlucky."

"I am not worried about you." Sharla sipped her drink slowly. "You will land on your feet."

"How?" Elsa growled. "I applied to all the advertising agencies in Kingston, every single one, including Magnus Communication and I swore I wouldn't apply there. I even went to Toddy with hat in hand, begging for him to use his connections."

"And?" Sharla asked.

"And nothing…" Elsa widened her eyes. "Nothing at all. I can't believe, Geo King is so powerful that he could blacklist me so thoroughly. I kind of had a small hope that because I knew Mason, I could get a foot in at his company but even there I have no luck."

"Mason Magnus? Sharla asked. "I can't believe you applied, and he said no."

"I don't know if he knows. His company is big, and he has an HR department." Elsa heaved a deep sigh. "I sent my resume through the regular channels. I felt kind of weird applying in the first place. He has this vendetta with Toddy."

"But not you," Sharla said shrewdly. "Mason likes you."

"No, he doesn't," Elsa snorted. "He has called me a wild cat. An untamed shrew. An untamable slip of a girl who will do anything for thrills. And that was within my hearing. Can you imagine when I am not around?"

Sharla grinned, "And what did you call him in return?"

"Boring. Bug-eyed twerp. Creep. Psychopath." Elsa sighed. "And plenty more, we have known each other for years. He makes me uncomfortable."

"Why?" Sharla got up and headed to the kitchen.

"Because…" Elsa shrugged. "I don't know. When Toddy was married to his mom, he would come over sometimes for the weekends, and he was silent for most of the time, which was creepy. Sometimes I would catch him looking at me. He doesn't do it to anybody else. He'd sit and look at me, not Giselle, not Tiana. Me."

"And I say again he liked you or was fascinated with you." Sharla looked in the fridge. "Why do you have so much take-out?"

"Went to a party at the Waterfalls," Elsa grunted. "There was more food than people."

"Okay." Sharla rummaged around in the fridge and finally pulled out a container. "If you really wanted a job, you'd call Mason, take advantage of his fascination."

"He is not fascinated with me. Not the way you think." Elsa snorted. "What I didn't tell you was that I was extremely mean to him in the past. I did stuff to make him react."

"Like what?" Sharla put the dish in the microwave and turned to Elsa. "Whatever could you have done?"

"I er." Elsa looked away shyly. "I used to…I haven't told anyone this."

“What?” Sharla asked, “what on earth did you do to poor Mason?”

“I would strip for him, dance while I was doing it, and then one time I kind of…well, I knew he was watching, and I can’t say it out loud. Let’s just say I was naked, and I knew he was sneaking around upstairs. I pleasured myself gave him an eyeful with lots of noise and then…”

“Then what?” Sharla gasped.

“He stopped coming by the house after that. I think I broke him.”

“Suppose he had raped you?” Sharla had a horrified expression on her face, “How old were you?”

“Sixteen.” Elsa sighed. “Or fifteen, what does it matter?”

“What does it matter?” Sharla widened her eyes, “You can’t egg a man on like that. What on earth possessed you?”

“Myrna said he was a virgin and was waiting for marriage. I couldn't believe it. He is a man. In my experience, men don't wait for marriage. I am more used to Toddy's type of man. You know loads of women, all the time. So I wanted to test Mason to see if it were true.”

“Good Lord help my wayward niece,” Sharla said dramatically.

“He passed the test.” Elsa frowned. “Maybe he doesn’t have anything down there. Maybe he is a eunuch. Maybe he lost his thing in an accident. Or maybe he is impotent. Have you thought of that?”

The microwave pinged announcing that it had finished the cycle. Sharla ignored it and shook her head. "No, I haven't thought of that. Elsa Cara Pryce…”

“Don’t worry about it.” Elsa waved off her aunt. “I cured him from staring at me like a zombie. He doesn't look me in the eyes anymore, and I think he avoids me at all cost. Three months ago, I went to the industry thing, where Geo King, my boss, tried to kiss me, and I broke his nose."

Sharla sighed. "You are lucky Geo didn't press charges."

"I wish he had." Elsa snarled, "then we could have the true story floating around, I hate the one he has been telling people, that I came on to him blah blah blah. All boring and untrue.

"Anyway, Mason gave a good talk, I know he saw me, I went close to him to say hello, and he blanked me, the twerp.

"Though I can't call him a twerp anymore. He has changed. You should see him now. He has grown into his looks. He gives me a Lance Gross kind of vibe."

"I can't believe what you did." Sharla still looked shocked. "What kind of behavior was that? You better thank God, it was Mason, a principled man and not anyone else."

"We all do stupid things when we were younger." Elsa sighed, "I can't take it back now. It was nearly ten years ago. Now I just want to be employed. I may be desperate enough to call Mason about hiring me..."

OTHER BOOKS BY BRENDA BARRETT

Pryce Sisters Series

Baby For A Pryce (Book 1)- Giselle Pryce had a bright future, two scholarships from Ivy League schools and a track career that was going somewhere, when she discovered she was pregnant. She had several decisions to make.

Right Pryce Wrong Time (Book 2)- Tiana got her high school teacher James fired for inappropriate conduct because of her jealousy. When she meets him again as an adult in a different situation, she has no idea how to act.

Yours, For A Pryce (Book 3)- Toddy Pryce offers his favorite sister Elsa to his young political rival Mason Magnus in exchange to not run against him in the next elections.

Wiley Brothers Series

Between Brothers (Book 0)- The beginning of the Wiley brothers saga, Joseph Wiley's unconventional family life may prove to be fatal to some members of the family.

For Pete's Sake (Book 1)- Preston has a run in with a child named Pete who claims that he is the grandson of their former housekeeper Pamela Stone.

Crossing Jordan (Book 2)- Jordan is miffed when Shawn takes her new fiancé to Jamaica and insists that he be man of honor at their wedding.

Fire and Walter (Book 3)- Walter's past came rushing to greet him shortly after his appointment as church elder. The new pastor was his childhood molestor, his wife was his ex from college and her cousin was the girl who got away. Walter had a lot of decisions to make.

The Perfect Guy (Book 4) - After a patient five years waiting for Lucia, Guy had his work cut out for him to prove himself worthy of her affections. He had played the part of poor farmer for too long and now he had competition in the form of the handsome doctor Ace Jackson.

The Patience of A Saint (Book 5)- Something was wrong with Saint's wife Sandrene. It didn't take a genius to see that she was changed beyond all recognition. Saint had to get to the bottom of it, before it was too late for them to salvage anything from the relationship.

A Case of Love (Book 6)- After a concert, Case is offered a girl to buy. Her fate was in his hands. He could keep her or leave her to the mercy of her evil family.

Resetter Series

Never Too Late (Book 1)- Addi finds out she is a resetter and goes back to the summer of 92 to change her family's lives.

Never Say Never (Book 2)- Skyler's handsome college lecturer, who happens to be her neighbor, has a 't' in his palms. Should she tell him the significance of it. If she does, would he believe her?

Now or Never (Book 3)- Ten years later Addi and Randy meet again at Randy's engagement party. Why is it that the chemistry between them was still so potent? Can they ever have a future together? Would Randy choose her this time around?

Almost Never (Book 4)- Tech genius Joshua Porter had all but given up on love. He then meets Portia, an inmate at the female penitentiary and his life takes a turn for the adventurous.

The Scarlett Family Series

Scarlett Baby (Book 1)- When the head of the Scarlett family died, Yuri had to return home to Treasure Beach for the funeral. What he didn't count on was seeing Marla, his childhood sweetheart and his best friend's wife. And when emotions overwhelm them and a few months later Marla is pregnant, Yuri wants the impossible: his best friend's wife and the baby they made together...

Scarlett Sinner (Book 2)- Pastor Troy Scarlett realizes the hard way that some sins are bound to be revealed, like the child that he had out of wedlock with his wife's mortal enemy from college. His wife Chelsea was not happy with the status quo. She was not taking care of the son of the woman she had so despised from college. And she could not get over the deep betrayal that she felt from her husband's indiscretion.

Scarlett Secret (Book 3)- Terri Scarlett had a soft spot for her friend, Lola. She was funny and sweet and they looked remarkably alike. But when Lola's Arab prince demands his bride, Terri foolishly exchange places with her friend and they meet up on a world of trouble.

Scarlett Love (Book 4)- Slater always looked forward to delivering packages to the law firm where he could get a glimpse of the stunning female lawyer, Amoy Gardener. Unfortunately, for Slater a woman like Amoy would not take him seriously, especially when she found out that he could not read!

Scarlett Promise (Book 5)- Driven by desperation Lisa Barclay decides to make some extra money by prostituting herself after being kicked out in the streets. Her first customer turns out to be a popular government senator and then to her horror he dies...

Scarlett Bride (Book 6)- When Oliver Scarlett's missionary work in the Congo region was coming to an end, he had a decision to make, marry Ashaki Azanga and save her from being the fourth wife to the chief of the village or leave her to her fate and get on with his life...

Scarlett Heart (Book 7)- After receiving a heart transplant shy librarian Noah Scarlett started to take on character traits that were unlike him and he kept dreaming of a girl named Cassandra Green...

Rebound Series

On The Rebound- For Better or Worse, Brandon vowed to stay with Ashley, but when worse got too much he moved out and met Nadine. For the first time in years he felt happy, but then Ashley remembered her wedding vows...

On The Rebound 2- Ashley reinvented herself and was now a first lady in a country church in Primrose Hill, but her obsessed ex friend Regina showed up and started digging into the lives of the saints at church. Somebody didn't like Regina's digging. Someone had secrets that were shocking enough to kill for...

Magnolia Sisters

Dear Mystery Guy (Book 1)- Della Gold details her life in a journal dedicated to a mystery guy. But when fascination turns into obsession she finds herself wanting to learn even more about him but in her pursuit of the mystery guy she begins to learn more about herself...

Bad Girl Blues (Book 2)- Brigid Manderson wanted to go to med school but for the time being she was an escort working for her mother, an ex-prostitute. When her latest customer offers her the opportunity of a lifetime would she take it? Or would she choose the harder path and uncertain love with a Christian guy?

Her Mistaken Dreams (Book 3)- Caitlin Denvers dream guy had serious issues. He has a dead wife in his past and he was the main suspect in her murder. Did he really do it? Or did Caitlin for the first time have a mistaken dream?

Just Like Yesterday (Book 4)- Hazel Brown lost six months of memory including the summer that she conceived her son, and had no idea who his father could bc. Now that she had the means to fight to get him back from the Deckers, she finds out that the handsome Curtis Decker is willing to share her son with her after all.

New Song Series

Going Solo (Book 1)- Carson Bell, had a lovely voice, a heart of gold, and was no slouch in the looks department. So why did Alice abandon him and their daughter? What did she want after ten years of silence?

Duet on Fire (Book 2)- Ian and Ruby had problems trying to conceive a child. If that wasn't enough, her ex-lover the current pastor of their church wants her back...

Tangled Chords (Book 3)- Xavier Bell, the poor, ugly duckling has made it rich and his looks have been incredibly improved too. Farrah Knight, hotel heiress had cruelly rejected him in the past but now she needed help. Could Xavier forgive and forget?

Broken Harmony(Book 4)- Aaron Lee, wanted the top job in his family company but he had a moral clause to consider just when Alka, his married ex-girlfriend walks back into his life.

A Past Refrain (Book 5)- Jayce had issues with forgetting Haley Greenwald even though he had a new woman in his life. Will he ever be able to shake his love for Haley?

Perfect Melody (Book 6)- Logan Moore had the perfect wife, Melody but his secretary Sabrina was hell bent on breaking up the family. Sabrina wanted Logan whatever the cost and she had a secret about Melody, that could shatter Melody's image to everyone.

The Bancroft Family Series

Homely Girl (Book 0) **-** April and Taj were opposites in so many ways. He was the cute, athletic boy that everybody wanted to be friends with. She was the overweight, shy, and withdrawn girl. Do April and Taj have a love that can last a lifetime? Or will time and separate paths rip them apart?

Saving Face (Book 1) **-** Mount Faith University drama begins with a dead president and several suspects including the president in waiting Ryan Bancroft.

Tattered Tiara (Book 2) - Micah Bancroft is targeted by femme fatale Deidra Durkheim. There are also several rape cases to be solved.

Private Dancer (Book 3) Adrian Bancroft was gutted when he returned to Jamaica and found out that his first and only love Cathy Taylor was a stripper and was literally owned by the menacing drug lord, Nanjo Jones.

Goodbye Lonely (Book 4) **-** Kylie Bancroft was shy and had to resort to going to confidence classes. How could she win the love of Gareth Beecher, her faculty adviser, a man with a jealous ex-wife in his past and a current mystery surrounding a hand found in his garden?

Practice Run (Book 5) **-** Marcus Bancroft had many reasons to avoid Mount Faith but Deidra Durkheim was not one of them. Unfortunately, on one of his visits he was the victim of a deliberate hit and run.

Sense of Rumor (Book 6) **-** Arnella Bancroft was the wild, passionate Bancroft, the creative loner who didn't mind living dangerously; but when a terrible thing happened to her at her friend Tracy's party, it changed her. She found that courting rumors can be devastating and that only the truth could set her free.

A Younger Man (Book 7)- Pastor Vanley Bancroft loved Anita Parkinson despite their fifteen-year age gap, but Anita had a secret, one that she could not reveal to Vanley. To tell him would change his feelings toward her, or force him to give up the ministry that he loved so much.

Just To See Her (Book 8)- Jessica Bancroft had the opportunity to meet her fantasy guy Khaled, he was finally coming to Mount Faith but she had feelings for Clay Reid, a guy who had all the qualities she was looking for. Who would she choose and what about the weird fascination Khaled had for Clay?

The Three Rivers Series

Private Sins (Book 1)- Kelly, the first lady at Three Rivers Church was pregnant for the first elder of her church. Could she keep the secret from her husband and pretend that all was well?

Loving Mr. Wright (Book 2)- Erica saw one last opportunity to ditch her single life when Caleb Wright appeared in her town. He was perfect for her, but what was he hiding?

Unholy Matrimony (Book 3) - Phoebe had a problem, she was poor and unhappy. Her solution to marry a rich man was derailed along the way with her feelings for Charles Black, the poor guy next door.

If It Ain't Broke (Book 4)- Chris Donahue wanted a place in his child's life. Pinky Black just wanted his love. She also wanted him to forget his obsession with Kelly and love her. That shouldn't be so hard? Should it?

Contemporary Romance/Drama

After The End--Torn between two lovers. Colleen married her high school sweetheart, Isaiah, hoping that they would live happily ever after but life intruded and Isaiah disappeared at sea. She found work with the rich and handsome, Enrique Lopez, as a housekeeper and realized that she couldn't keep him at arms length...

Love Triangle: Three Sides To The Story- George, the husband, Marie, the wife and Karen-the mistress. They all get to tell their side of the story.

The Preacher And The Prostitute - Prostitution and the clergy don't mix. Tell that to ex-prostitute, Maribel, who finds herself in love with the Pastor at her church. Can an ex-prostitute and a pastor have a future together?

New Beginnings - Inner city girl Geneva was offered an opportunity of a lifetime when she found out that her 'real' father was a very wealthy man. Her decision to live up-town meant that she had to leave Froggie, her 'ghetto don,' behind. She also found herself battling with her stepmother and battling her emotions for Justin, a suave up-towner.

Full Circle- After graduating from university, Diana

wanted to return to Jamaica to find her siblings. What she didn't foresee was that she would meet Robert Cassidy and that both their pasts would be intertwined, and that disturbing questions would pop up about their parentage, just when they were getting close.

Historical Fiction/Romance

The Empty Hammock- Workaholic, Ana Mendez, fell asleep in a hammock and woke up in the year 1494. It was the time of the Tainos, a time when life seemed simpler, but Ana knew that all of that was about to change.

The Pull Of Freedom- Even in bondage the people, freshly arrived from Africa, considered themselves free. Led by Nanny and Cudjoe the slaves escaped the Simmonds' plantation and went in different directions to forge their destiny in the new country called Jamaica.

Jamaican Comedy (Material contains Jamaican dialect)

Di Taxi Ride And Other Stories- Di Taxi Ride and Other Stories is a collection of twelve witty and fast paced short stories. Each story tells of a unique slice of Jamaican life.

www.ingramcontent.com/pod-product-compliance
Ingram Content Group UK Ltd.
Pitfield, Milton Keynes, MK11 3LW, UK
UKHW021650190726
13853UKWH00001B/165

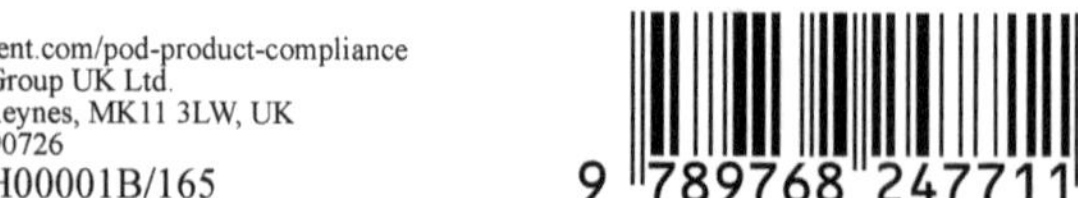

9 789768 247711